THE GIRL IN THE PICTURE

THE
GIRL
IN THE
PICTURE

ALEXANDRA MONIR

DELACORTE PRESS

Text copyright © 2016 by Alexandra Monir
Jacket art copyright © 2016 by Arcangel Images and Shutterstock

"Lovesong"
Words and Music by Robert Smith, Laurence Tolhurst, Simon Gallup,
Paul S. Thompson, Boris Williams and Roger O'Donnell
Copyright © 1989 by Fiction Songs Ltd.
All Rights in the U.S. and Canada Administered by Universal Music - MGB Songs
International Copyright Secured. All Rights Reserved.
Reprinted by Permission of Hal Leonard Corporation.

"Tomorrow Is My Turn"
Words and Music by Charles Aznavour, Marcel Stellman, and Yves Stephanie
Copyright © 1967 LES ED. FRENCH MUSIC
Copyright renewed.
All Rights Administered by Universal Music Corp.
All Rights Reserved. Used by permission.
Reprinted by Permission of Hal Leonard LLC.

randomhouseteens.com

Educators and librarians, for a variety of teaching tools, visit us at
RHTeachersLibrarians.com

Library of Congress Cataloging-in-Publication Data
Names: Monir, Alexandra, author.
Title: The girl in the picture / Alexandra Monir.
Description: First edition. | New York : Delacorte Press, 2016. | Summary: When a popular high school boy is found murdered, everyone is surprised he carried pictures of himself with Nicole Morgan, a shy "music geek" no one knew was close to him.
Identifiers: LCCN 2015042550 | ISBN 978-0-385-74390-7 (hc) |
ISBN 978-0-385-37252-7 (ebook)
Subjects: | CYAC: Murder—Fiction. | Secrets—Fiction. | High schools—Fiction. | Schools—Fiction. | Disfigured persons—Fiction. | Mystery and detective stories.
Classification: LCC PZ7.M7495 Gir 2016 | DDC [Fic]—dc23

The text of this book is set in 12-point Dante.

Printed in the United States of America
10 9 8 7 6 5 4 3 2 1
First Edition

PART ONE
Lana + Chace

PROLOGUE

CHACE
OCTOBER 24, 2016

At first it's no more than a blurry shape on the ground, large enough to beat me up, slow enough for me to escape from. Then my focus clears, and I see why the body won't move. Its limbs are tangled and twisted among the fallen leaves. Blood spills over the sleeves of a well-worn varsity jacket, and a once-familiar face has turned gray, its mouth frozen on its last word spoken. A word now ringing in my ears. *"You."*

I take a step closer, bracing for the gut-wrenching pain of recognition. But as I stare at my maimed self lying in the woods behind the soccer field—*my* soccer field—there is no pain. No emotion at all, really. I guess I shouldn't expect to feel anything. I'm dead.

Still, there is a flicker of something, an image—no, *images*. They push to the forefront of my mind, growing stronger the more I stare at my rigid body. Lips on lips, the sound of her voice calling after me, a sharp blade inches from my neck, the last face before it all went black. And then the realization dawns that I've seen this all before; that I knew this would happen if I chose her—if I strayed from the path laid out before me.

Footsteps. They're coming, mere seconds away from finding my body. Soon this section of the woods will be roped off with yellow tape, newscasters and Oyster Bay students all clamoring for a view of where I died. Then the detectives will swarm, full of theories and names.

I think I know who the first two names will be.

And yet, I have somewhere to go, don't I? An afterlife waiting to check me in?

But I can't go just yet.

I need a little longer, one more glimpse of her.

Before every trace of me turns to ash, I need to know the truth.

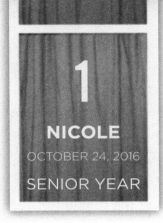

"Though some may reach for the stars,
Others will end behind bars."

The words play in my mind, my eyes closed as I dance the bow across the strings of the violin. She and I are a team, moving and breathing in unison, producing a sound that transforms this cold, lonely dorm room into a makeshift Carnegie Hall. A momentary paradise.

Some violins sound too bright, better suited to cheery occasions like Christmas concerts or wedding processionals. Not this one, a walnut-brown Maggini on loan from Professor Teller. It's full of dark tones and blue notes that grow icier as I move my bow closer and closer to the fingerboard.

It sounds like me.

My phone starts to vibrate, rattling against the desk, and

for a moment my hopes rise. But then I hear the tinny clanging bells and remember. It's only my stupid alarm clock.

I open my eyes, and without thinking, my gaze flicks toward the mirror on the opposite wall. Just like that, the spell is broken. I'm not the star violinist anymore. I'm the girl with the scar.

I turn away, switching my focus to the careful packing of my violin and cueing up a playlist on my iPhone, which launches with a whimsical, horn-drenched score by Alexandre Desplat. One of my favorites. The music steers me, nudging me through my morning routine. Lord knows I wouldn't be able to get up most days without it.

I keep my back to the mirror while I button the stiff white collared shirt emblazoned with Oyster Bay Prep's crest, and zip up the navy plaid skirt that cuts just above the knee. A navy jacket, kneesocks, and penny loafers complete the look, and for a moment I think I hear Lana's snickering voice. *"I bet you this uniform was dreamed up by a creepy old dude on faculty, indulging in some sort of schoolgirl fantasy."* She had a point there. I look about twelve years old in this getup, but my taller, better-endowed classmates might as well be playing dress-up for the cover of *Maxim*.

It's almost time to face myself, but first I wash up in the little sink I had installed in my room. Anything to not have to stand in line with the other fourth-floor girls, all of us brushing our teeth in unison while staring at our reflections. No, thank you. I'd rather just zip in and out whenever I have to use the toilet, keeping my head down until I'm back in the safety of my room, which Headmaster Higgins was sympathetic enough to let me keep as a single.

The clock flashes 7:50, and I know I can't put this off any longer. Grabbing a tube of my latest overpriced concealer, I turn to face the mirror.

In the initial weeks following the accident, I used to hold my breath and dream that it would be gone—that my face might have magically healed on its own, without any need for a surgery so expensive it would require Mom to file for bankruptcy. But I've learned my lesson since then. There's no such thing as an overnight miracle, and when I look now, the jagged edge is still ever present, running down my cheek like a frozen teardrop.

I examine my scar in the mirror, turning my head this way and that as I apply the concealer with its dainty little wand. With each new product I try, I can't help but hope that *this* will be the one that finally delivers on the advertising's promise: "Erase your most unsightly blemish!"

Yeah, right. All this concealer manages to do is tint the scar orange. But it doesn't matter. Even if I did manage to cover the scar, it would still be there—still the first thing they saw whenever they looked at me, the rumors of That Night forever associated with my name.

It's funny, because I never even used to care how I looked. All that mattered was how well I played. I guess it's true what they say, that you don't miss something until it's gone—

because the day I transformed from a decently attractive girl into the Phantom of the Opera's sister was the day my wildly ambitious dreams devolved into just one: to look normal . . . or maybe even pretty.

With a sigh, I hoist my schoolbag over my shoulder and stick my earbuds into my ears. It's time to leave the little haven of Room #403.

I open my door to the typical morning scene in the dorm hall: bleary-eyed girls yawning their way into the bathroom with toiletry bags in hand, their type-A counterparts thundering down the stairs as though they're ten minutes late instead of early. The social butterflies are darting in and out of each other's rooms, taking selfies and trading accessories, and it's hard to believe that for a minute I was one of them.

Even with my headphones on, I can hear two of my classmates saunter up behind me, their conversation a low hum punctuated by a loud burst of laughter. I'd know that laugh anywhere. And that's when it happens—a sickening lurch in my stomach. A moment when my vision turns pixelated. A fuzzy memory pokes its way into my consciousness, edging out the music playing in my earbuds, and I can feel myself falling again, my body tumbling over a precipice, the earth scratching at my face.

I let myself sink down onto the top stair, ignoring the weird looks I'm surely receiving. *Inhale, exhale,* I chant silently, until the feeling of dread lifts, and Alexandre Desplat's horns and piano return to my ears.

It's just another day, Nicole, I remind myself. *You've gotten through it before. You'll get through it again.*

• • •

Oyster Bay Preparatory School is the kind of place you'd find in a Thomas Kinkade painting, with its quaint cobblestone walkways, lush lawns, redbrick walls, and arched windows. It oozes privilege and peace, a little bubble existing only for the fortunate ones who were good enough, smart enough, talented enough, to make it inside. You *had* to be the best to pass the entrance exams and get in. Okay, maybe a certain few didn't need to worry about that, but most of us did. So it's nearly impossible to walk through the velvet-carpeted hallways without feeling a twinge of pride, looking upon the portraits of presidents, artists, and geniuses lining the walls, luminaries who were once just like us, sitting in these same classroom seats. Sometimes I wonder if that's what keeps me here—the idea that one day, I could be a legend on the wall. At least in portraits, they can paint away any flaws.

The school is shaped like the letter H, with our sleeping quarters, known as the dorm wing, making up the left building. Joyce Hall of Music & Arts is on the right, while the adjoining wide structure between the two buildings is what the school brochure calls "the crux of it all," Academics Hall. You can probably guess which wing I'm most loyal to. My violin is the only reason I'm here.

My first class of the day is Biology: Genetics & Ethics, a

class I used to look forward to because of who I shared it with. But when I enter the classroom, shaking my hair in front of my face like armor, I notice one of the desks is empty.

Brianne Daly, the one friend I can still count on, gives my hand a squeeze as I slide into my seat next to hers.

"Hey. Notice something weird?" she asks.

My eyes fly to the empty desk.

"I mean, have we *ever* made it to class before Mr. Isaacs?"

That's true. Our biology teacher is a stickler for punctuality, so this is a first. The final bell rings, the minutes stretch on, and still no Mr. Isaacs. Brianne and I watch as the rest of the class celebrates this temporary freedom. Lizzie and Felix, the senior class's newest It Couple, take the opportunity to squeeze into one chair and make googly eyes at each other, while the social butterflies flit around their desks, talking loudly over one another to be heard above the Kendrick Lamar track blaring from Charlie Fields's portable speakers. No one wonders what's keeping our teacher. No one cares.

And then I feel Brianne nudge me in the ribs.

"Look at his face."

I follow her gaze to where Mr. Isaacs is finally walking through the door, his expression dumbstruck, as if in a daze. His trademark horn-rimmed glasses are missing, and as I take in the red blotches on his cheeks, I realize he's been crying. I can't look away. I've never seen an adult cry before. Mom always held it in, waited until she was behind the closed door of her room.

Mr. Isaacs reaches the podium in front of the whiteboard,

and for the first time he looks lost in his usual place. Charlie turns off the music, and without our teacher so much as saying a word, everyone takes their seats. My classmates might have been blissfully ignorant seconds ago, but it's clear from Mr. Isaacs's demeanor that this isn't going to be a normal school day. Not even close.

His mouth opens and closes twice before he finally finds his voice.

"I'm sorry—so sorry—for what I have to say." He takes a shaky breath, then stares straight ahead at a point on the wall. "One of your classmates, he . . . he was found dead early this morning."

I see Brianne's jaw drop, I hear the gasps around me, but my mind can't process it. And then Mr. Isaacs says a name.

"Chace Porter."

I'm dreaming this, of course. It's the worst kind of nightmare, but the sweetest relief will be mine when I wake up. I pinch myself so hard I nearly draw blood. Not dreaming.

A roar rises up from my stomach and chokes me. An animal inside struggles to get free, to hurl itself at the teacher and send claw marks gashing down his tearstained cheeks for telling us this lie, for making this mistake.

And then I feel her eyes burning a hole into my back—the girl who made me hate the social butterflies. I turn and meet her glance, taking in the frozen expression and trembling lower lip. Our classmates congregate around her, stricken and wailing, clueless that they are comforting the wrong person.

I stare down at the hardwood floor. Where are my sobs,

my screams? I can't seem to make a single noise, even though my cries are deafening in my mind.

Lana is still looking at me, and as the realization hits that he's gone, that she and I are all that's left from the mess of our triangle, I feel the desperate urge to crawl out of my skin and disappear. I jolt out of my seat and make for the door, blind to the police officer entering the classroom just as I'm making my escape.

And I run straight into the policeman's chest.

2

LANA

SEPTEMBER 7, 2015

JUNIOR YEAR

The second I spot him, I know. This is the boy I've been hearing about. He's there under the oak tree, oblivious to the rest of us, focused instead on juggling a soccer ball between his feet. I watch him, and something pulls at my chest.

I'm clearly not the only one who notices him. It seems like most of us returning juniors are putting on a show this afternoon, pretending to be interested in each other's summer stories, pretending we care, when we're really just staring through our sunglasses at the new guy. We never get boys like this at Oyster Bay Prep. Our male classmates are all the same: bland, blond sons of the patriarchy, with their old-money manners and hand-me-down sense of humor. None of them have a clue how to get you *really* interested—how to push you up against a wall and kiss you like they actually mean it. I can tell, just by watching this stranger with the soccer ball, he can. He's different—dark, muscular, with the body of a man, not a boy. His eyes have a glint to them, like someone dreaming up a wild dare. There's nothing too safe about those eyes, nothing familiar.

"Isn't that what's-his-name? You know, the congressman's son?"

Stephanie's voice snaps me back to reality. In just a few minutes, our headmaster will quit her long and boring welcome-back speech and the barbecue will begin. How many girls will make a beeline for the hot new guy, competing to be first, to be the one who gets to show him around campus? I'm not about to sit back and count.

"I'm going to go find out," I tell Stephanie with a fluff of my hair.

He looks up as I come closer, and I thank the Lord we didn't have to wear our lame uniforms to the barbecue. My silk romper is so much more flattering, with its deep V-neck, figure-skimming shorts, and sapphire shade that sets off my bronze skin and dark hair. I catch his eyes roving over me appreciatively, not in the creepy way of men wolf-whistling through their car windows, but in the way I always imagined my future boyfriend would look at me. Like he can't believe his luck.

"Hi. I'm Lana Rivera." I hold out my hand, giving him my best flirty smile. "I'm guessing you're a transfer?"

As if I didn't already know.

"Hello, Lana Rivera." He flashes me a grin as he shakes my hand, and a dimple appears in each of his cheeks. "Yeah, I just transferred from St. John's in DC. I'm Chace Porter."

"So, what made you leave DC? Running from something?" I joke.

He laughs, his face flushing. I take a step closer, noticing the color of his eyes. They're a bluer gray than they appeared from afar, a shock of brightness against his olive skin and brown hair.

"I'm here because of soccer, actually," he replies. "Your school recruited me."

Knew that already. I bite my lip, considering whether to go for the blatant flirting or keep it coy. I go for the flirting.

"Well. It looks like our school got lucky."

My efforts are rewarded. Chace breaks into another smile, bigger than the first, and it gives me a bubbling feeling in my stomach, a sensation I can't remember experiencing since I was a kid ready to rip open a present on Christmas morning.

"Looks like I got pretty lucky myself, meeting a total knockout on my first day."

His eyes twinkle, and there go those dimples again. I suck in my breath. This is happening.

"You've got some good karma working for you," I say, aiming for a breezy tone. "Especially since I was just about to offer to show you the ropes around here."

"Really? That sounds *much* better than getting the tour from Mrs. Braymore."

Chace brushes his hand against my arm, and it's so quick and casual that I can't tell if it's on purpose or by accident. I look at Stephanie and the other girls, hoping they saw. Of course they did. The word will spread quickly now. The new guy may be the most intriguing prospect to set foot on Oyster Bay grounds since we all arrived as freshmen, but just like that, he's off-limits. I got to him first.

"Come on," I say, giving him a gentle nudge. "Let me introduce you to everyone."

We leave the oak tree and join my friends, just in time for the end of Headmaster Higgins's speech and the beginning of the barbecue. As we cross the South Lawn, I envision the rest of the afternoon. Chace and I will wait in line for food together, then we'll sit next to each other at the picnic tables, laughing as barbecue sauce drips onto our fingers and our knees touch beneath the table.

If I play my cards right, it'll only be a matter of time before he's mine.

• • •

He keeps a polite space between us as I lead him through the trail of cherry trees, over the little wooden bridge, and down toward the quadrangle of redbrick campus buildings.

"Let me see your class schedule. I'll let you know if you got screwed or not."

Chace hands me a folded paper from his back pocket, and I give it a quick scan.

"AP English, damn. So you're an athlete *and* a smarty?" I raise an eyebrow at him over the top of the paper.

His face flushes again, and I feel a small burst of triumph at the realization that he's nervous around me. Or shy. Or something.

"Latin III with Ms. Garcia," I continue reading. "That's one class we have in common. I've got to warn you, it's a pain in the ass."

"Noted," Chace says with a nod, the dimples reappearing in his cheeks. "So, everything is in this building here, right?" He nods up at Academics Hall.

"All your typical classes are, but music and arts are in Joyce Hall, where the theater is," I explain. "And of course, PE is either on the field or at the pool, depending on whether you have swimming or field sports."

"Yeah, I noticed a Choral Music class on my schedule," Chace says with a grimace. "Is that, like, mandatory here?"

I roll my eyes. I feel his pain.

"Until senior year, it is. Oyster Bay goes after musicians and artsy types the same way it recruits athletes like you. They're basically fishing for maximum celebrity alumni. Only a few get into the Virtuoso Program, but they still force even the most untalented to take at least one performing arts class through junior year, I guess on the off chance they might discover someone." I shrug. "Come on, let me show you how to get to your classes. Academics Hall is kind of a labyrinth."

He closes the space between us by a hair as we walk

through the mahogany double doors. A high-ceilinged foyer welcomes us, its walls lined with banners and trophy cases dating back to the last century, pointing the way toward the first cluster of classrooms. Only the nerdiest among us could be found studying on our day off, before term has even started, but of course there are a few stragglers in the building, eyes sunken from reviewing who-knows-what all morning.

As I give Chace the grand tour, I feel oddly like I'm on a stage, all too aware of everything I'm saying, of the inflections of my voice. I'm only talking about teachers, classes, and the best shortcut from Algebra III to Physics II; it's hardly high-stakes stuff. This should be easy. I can flirt with my eyes closed. But something about the way this new guy looks at me, as though there's only good to be found, makes my temperature rise. And I want to be done with this tour charade. I want more.

My phone vibrates in my purse, and I pull it out while Chace is busy peering at all the high-tech equipment in the science lab. It's a text from Mom.

Met him yet?

I quickly hit delete. I'm not doing this for her. I'm doing this for me.

"Hey, Chace?" I call out. "Let's go to Joyce Hall. I know you're not into the artsy-fartsy stuff either, but trust me, you'll want to see the theater."

"Sounds good." Chace falls into step beside me, and we head out of Academics Hall and back into the quad. The sun is setting, casting a golden-pink hue across the grass. Oyster Bay Prep has never looked more perfect, like a movie set, and for a moment I feel like the leading lady with something thrilling on the horizon. I can't help it—I break into a run and turn a cartwheel across the lawn.

Chace applauds as he catches up to me. "I give that a ten out of ten, Lana Rivera."

I dip into a playful curtsy. We're in front of Joyce Hall now, which would be indistinguishable from Academics if not for the four marble columns flanking its front steps. The grandeur of those columns seems to lord power over the other buildings, as if saying *this* is the special place, this is where the real treasure is found.

"Wow," Chace remarks as we step inside, our shoes practically sinking into the plush red carpeting. "It's easy to see which department Oyster Bay prizes most."

"They definitely classed it up in here," I agree. "But just wait till you see the theater. That's clearly where all the alumni bribe-money must have gone."

Chace laughs, a warm, infectious sound that makes me want to keep the joke going. Of course, we both know I wasn't joking. There's something about having parents in politics that exposes you to the truth early on in life, and alumni bribes? That's reality. It's the reason—if we're being brutally honest—why I got into this school.

We're nearing the theater now, but as we reach the doors, the sound of a violin emanates from behind them. I turn to Chace with a disappointed shrug.

"I guess there's a rehearsal or something going on in there."

Chace steps closer, pressing his ear against the door.

"I know that song. Let's go in and watch."

"Um . . . okay."

Now it's my turn to follow as he pushes open the theater doors and strides down the aisle until we're shuffling into the second row of seats, looking up at a girl on the stage who doesn't even know we're there.

I glance at Chace. He doesn't seem to notice the magnificence of the theater; he isn't making the typical awed remarks about the chandeliered ceiling and gilded stage. He's not even looking. His eyes are almost closed as he listens to the music, a half smile forming on his face, as if remembering something. A twinge of irritation flashes through me.

I study the girl currently capturing Chace's attention. She might be talented, but thankfully she's not hot. Her sandy blond hair is in desperate need of frizz control, and I'm slightly horrified to see that she's wearing denim overalls. *Overalls.* I know some people would like to think they're coming back in style, but—no.

The song must be over now, because Chace has leaped to his feet clapping, and the girl is blinking her eyes open, her cheeks turning tomato-red with surprise when she sees us.

"Oh God. I—I thought I was alone in here," she stammers. "So embarrassing—"

I roll my eyes. *Please.*

"Are you kidding? That was amazing," Chace raves. "Was that—were you playing the song from *The Godfather II?*"

I cough to disguise my snort of laughter. So we weren't even listening to *real* classical music?

Violin Chick smiles, and it's the wide, showing-all-her-teeth kind of smile that lets me know she has *not* learned the art of seduction.

"Yes!" she exclaims. "By Nino Rota. It's 'The Immigrant Theme' from the movie. How did you know?"

"I watched all the *Godfather* movies with my dad when I was little. I was probably way too young," Chace says with a chuckle. "But anyway, they're still my favorites."

"Those movies have the best music," Violin Chick says, still beaming. "Film scores are kind of my thing."

Okay, enough already. I stand up, reasserting my place next to Chace.

"I'm Lana Rivera, and this is—"

"Lana Rivera?" Violin Chick interrupts, her smile growing even wider. Who knew *that* was possible.

"Yep, that's me. And this is Chace Porter. Are you a transfer?"

"No." She lets out an awkward giggle. "I'm Nicole Morgan. We had a couple classes together freshman year."

"Oh *yeah*. I remember," I lie.

"But anyway, this is such a coincidence, because I was hoping to see you before," she continues.

"See me before what?" I ask. I'm really getting wary of this weirdo.

"Before move-in." When my expression remains blank, Nicole adds, "I'm your new dormmate!"

Wrong. I force a polite expression onto my face.

"You must be mistaken. I'm rooming with Stephanie Sparks, just like last year."

"Headmaster Higgins switched up the room assignments for this year. Didn't you see it in the welcome packet? She wrote something about 'injecting new life into our social cliques.'"

I grit my teeth. This can't be happening. I'm *not* being separated from my best friend and forced to share a bedroom with a socially inept music nerd.

"That's awesome," Chace says, grinning at me. "You'll get your own private concert whenever you want."

Yeah. Awesome, all right. But I can't let Chace see how pissed off I am.

"Good point." I fix a smile on my face. "I can't wait."

3

NICOLE

OCTOBER 24, 2016

"What the future has in store,
No one ever knows before."

"Hold on one moment, miss. No one's leaving just yet."

I glance up at the figure blocking my escape, and my stomach seizes. He's wearing the telltale dark blue uniform and matching peaked cap, ammunition slung like a warning in his patrol belt. The sight of a police officer at the front of the classroom only amplifies this nightmare, and I look desperately to the door, aching to be alone, to scream and sob and try to make sense of all of this in private.

The cop does a double take when he looks at me. It's my scar, of course. That's the only reason anyone ever looks twice in my direction now. But I don't care anymore. The one person I wanted to look pretty for is gone. Let me be a hideous monster for the rest of my life—if it would only bring him back.

Mr. Isaacs steps in front of me, extending his hand to the cop.

"Morning, Officer," he says, with a grim shake of his head. "Unthinkable, isn't it?"

The room starts to spin, pins and needles pricking at my insides, and for a moment I don't know where I am. Then I hear fragments of the cop's words.

"A terrible loss . . . We're doing everything we can. . . . need to speak to your students about the case."

Mr. Isaacs finally notices me standing alongside them, my foot tapping against the linoleum floor like a soundtrack to my panic.

"Nicole, I need you back in your seat."

But I can't move. Brianne appears at my arm, looking at me strangely as she leads me back to our desks.

"Are you okay, Nicole? You look like you're going to faint."

Before I can answer, Mr. Isaacs turns to address the class.

"Everyone, I'm going to have to ask that you all please take a seat and give Officer Ladge your undivided attention."

A nervous hush comes over the room, the kind only a police officer can inspire. Everyone makes their way back to their desks except Lana, who remains crumpled in a ball, sobbing, Stephanie and Kara at her side. The old instinct of friendship kicks in and I turn around in my seat to meet her eyes—but just as quickly, I remember, and turn back to the front of the room.

Officer Ladge steps forward.

"Let me begin by saying how deeply sorry I am for the loss of your classmate and friend. I know Chace Porter was a beloved member of the community here, and his loss will be tremendously felt. To that end, we've arranged for grief counselors to be on-site all week. Please take the time to speak with them. It will help." The officer clears his throat. "But I'm afraid there's more. The specifics of how Mr. Porter was found, and in what condition, lead us to believe foul play was involved."

Foul play? The words swim in my head, making no sense.

"Do you mean . . . like, it wasn't an accident? He was killed?" a petrified voice I recognize as Grace Levin's calls out.

The officer pauses for a split second.

"Yes. Based on the evidence and the state of the body, we can confirm that this was a murder."

My heart slips out of my chest as he speaks. I can practically see it flopping about pathetically on the classroom floor, ready to be stomped on and torn apart by all the feet in this room. The officer's voice seems distorted as he resumes his speech, like a hideous recording played in slow motion.

"Our findings show that Chace was last seen alive during the early-morning hours yesterday at the off-campus party thrown by Tyler Hemming. Mr. Hemming is cooperating with us and putting together a list of everyone who attended. We'll need to interview each of you who was there."

I wasn't supposed to be at the party. I wasn't invited. But when I got the text, I couldn't hold myself back. And now my mind can't stop replaying the argument and the kiss, memories that are like shots to the gut now that I know they were our last. There are gaps, too—pockets of haze and time-jumps within the night that I know are the result of gulping down Tyler's signature drink when it was handed to me. I didn't feel the effects until later, when it was too late.

"We'll need to speak with those closest to Mr. Porter first. Nicole Morgan, if you can please come with me—"

His words set off a bomb. A collective shock ripples through the room, with audible gasps and a smattering of nervous laughter culminating in a flurry of outraged voices as my classmates talk over one another, all of them rushing to clear up Officer Ladge's blunder. I know what they're thinking. *How could he think she, of all people, was closest to Chace?* Brianne stares at me, confusion written across her face.

One prickly voice cuts above the others, like a knife.

"I was his girlfriend. He barely even knew her."

Officer Ladge looks taken aback, frowning as he glances from me to Lana and back again. I hold my breath. This isn't happening.

"I apologize, Miss . . . ?"

"Lana Rivera," Mr. Isaacs murmurs to the officer.

"Miss Rivera. If you'll come with me, we can speak in private, and I'll be glad to arrange any help you might need during this difficult time." The officer's eyes flick to me again and I shift in my seat, wondering how he knew my name, how he could have guessed about me and Chace.

"I can't." Lana's voice breaks. "I can't do this, I can't believe this."

The officer, clearly trained for horrendous moments such as these, swoops to her side, helping her to her feet. I watch along with the rest of the class as he places a comforting hand on her back and steers her to the door, muttering something to Mr. Isaacs out of the corner of his mouth just before they leave.

"All of you who attended the party this weekend, I expect you to cooperate with the authorities and answer any questions they might have." Mr. Isaacs wrings his hands, looking hopelessly out of his depth in these murky waters. "In the meantime, please take the day to . . . to comfort and be good to each other. Grief counselors will be on the premises for the rest of the week, so please do take advantage—"

I feel the bile rising in my throat. Sweat drenches my brow and I know I'm on the verge of being sick, or having a panic attack—or both. I push out of my chair, ignoring Brianne calling after me, and make for the door. But this time it's Mr. Isaacs blocking my path.

"I'm sorry, Nicole. The officer does still need to talk to you. He asked me to . . ." My teacher swallows uncomfortably. "To not let you leave."

• • •

The classroom has thinned out, and now it's down to me and Mr. Isaacs. The other students all received his permission to go back to their dorms, to call their parents, to visit the grief counselors. Only I was forced to stay.

"You sure you don't want to come with me?" Brianne had asked, before leaving.

I shook my head, telling her I wanted to be alone. That was true enough. It was the other part I hoped to keep hidden—what the officer must know. What he thinks *I* know. During the hour waiting for him, I caught my mind descending into thoughts of self-preservation, and they sent a flush of shame to my cheeks, that I even cared about my own stupid life and reputation when Chace was . . . *No*. I won't let myself believe the word *dead*.

"Miss Morgan."

My head jerks forward. Officer Ladge is back, but this time he's joined by a beady-eyed woman in a gray pantsuit, her hair pulled back in a stiff bun.

"This is Detective Jillian Kimble," Officer Ladge says, gesturing to the woman now looming over my desk.

"We have some questions for you," Detective Kimble says briskly. "We don't want to take up any more of your teacher's time, so we'll go down to the headmaster's office to chat."

This sounds like yet another bad sign in a morning riddled with them. I force myself to get up, to put one wobbly foot in front of the other until I'm in the doorway with them, the third point of a terrifying triangle.

The officer and the detective lead the way out of the classroom and down the two flights of stairs to Headmaster Higgins's office, as if they've taken this route dozens of times. I wonder if I should call my mom, if I can insist on having a parent with me when I talk to these two. Then again, that might make me seem nervous—like I have something to hide.

Headmaster Higgins is sitting at her desk, head in her hands, when we enter the office. She stands quickly when she sees the uniformed pair with me, then wraps me in a hug. I let myself lean on her shoulder for an extra moment.

"Nicole, dear, how are you holding up?"

I can only shake my head. The headmaster turns to the officers.

"I don't mean to be impertinent, but could you have the wrong student? Nicole Morgan is the last person at Oyster Bay Prep I would have imagined being mixed up in anything like this."

"We just have a few routine questions," the detective says in her smooth tone. She pats the empty chair opposite the headmaster's desk. "Please have a seat, Nicole."

Once I'm in the chair, she leans forward, peering into my eyes as if trying to catch me in a lie.

"First things first. Were you at Tyler Hemming's party on Saturday night?"

I shut my eyes briefly.

"Yes."

"Did you see and speak to Chace Porter there?"

"Yes."

"Can you tell me about your interaction with him that night?"

No.

"It wasn't much. We said hi and I congratulated him on the soccer game. That was basically it."

Detective Kimble narrows her eyes, as if weighing my responses in her mind. Officer Ladge stands behind her, nodding emphatically every time she asks a question, as though Kimble is reading from a script he wrote.

"What time did you leave the party?" she presses.

I don't know. I don't remember. But of course, I can't say that.

"Around eleven," I answer.

She arches an eyebrow.

"The party apparently ended a couple of hours later. Why did you leave on the earlier side?"

I don't know how I'm supposed to respond. Can she tell that I'm holding something back? I touch my cheek, my fingers resting on the scar.

"I'm not the most popular girl at parties."

"But still you went," she says pointedly.

What is she getting at?

"Practically our whole class went. I didn't want to miss out."

"Nicole," she says, studying me like a hunter eyeing its prey. "Did you have a *romantic* relationship with Chace Porter?"

The question barrels in from out of the blue, catching me

off guard. For a moment I'm sure I misheard, until Detective Kimble repeats the question. "Were you romantically involved with Chace Porter?"

"We were friends," I respond, my voice breaking on the past tense.

"Just friends?" Officer Ladge gives me a sharp look, and my breath catches in my throat. I don't know how, but they know things they shouldn't—and now I have no choice but to tell them more than I want to reveal.

"We got close. But he had a girlfriend, and it . . . well, it didn't work out."

Headmaster Higgins comes to my defense.

"Officers, is this really the time to rehash perfectly normal adolescent drama? Miss Morgan is clearly in shock."

"The issue pertains to what we found at the scene of the crime. It currently plays a critical role in our investigation." Her eyes never leaving mine, Detective Kimble opens her briefcase and retrieves a small item wrapped in plastic. "This was in the victim's coat pocket when his body was found."

She places it on the headmaster's desk and I'm afraid to look, I can't bear another shot of pain. But then I catch the familiar edges of a photo-booth strip—and it's as if he's in this room with me, answering every question I've ever had.

I push out of my seat in a trance, leaning over the desk to gaze at the plastic-covered images. As I look down at our glowing faces from junior year, the sounds and sights of the happiest day of my life come rushing back to me. I can hear the whoosh of roller coasters and the shrieks of revelers; I can feel Chace's hand interlacing with mine as we step through the turnstiles into the Long Island Sound Memorial Day Carnival.

The sun beams down on us as the band begins playing a cheerful Disney tune, and I have the sudden desperate desire to bottle this moment—because this kind of perfect happiness can't possibly last forever. As if reading my mind, Chace nods toward a photo booth, situated between the lines for the Ferris wheel and the cotton candy cart.

"I think we need a souvenir from our first real date," he says with a grin. "What do you say?"

"Nicole? What do you have to say?"

The detective's brusque voice jars me out of my reverie. I blink, my mind joining my body back in this tense office, my eyes refocusing on the pictures in front of me.

In the top photo, I'm nestled in his lap like I belong there, my face lit by a soft smile while his lips rest on my shoulder. The second picture has us giddy, turning to each other instead of the camera, our faces crinkled with laughter. His hands are wrapped around my waist in this shot, while my palms press against his chest.

The last picture has always been my favorite—when we forgot the camera's existence entirely, and it froze us in a moment of unbridled affection. His head bent down as he whispered to me, his fingers cradling my chin. All I could do then was look up at him, my eyes filled with the wordless awe of being loved.

It was just an interlude, a crescendo in time, and before I was prepared for it to end, life swung back into its monotonous chorus. And then my accident happened, shattering any notion that the happiness in these photos was real or lasting.

I thought he'd forgotten this—us. I thought I was the only one holding it in, storing it for safekeeping in the most secret part of myself.

The detective clears her throat loudly.

"So can you explain to us, Miss Morgan, why the boyfriend of Lana Rivera had these photos of you two in his pocket when he died?"

I lie on my bed, arms folded as I watch my unexpected roommate putter around our dorm, folding dull-looking clothes and pinning up posters of wrinkly old violinists on her side of the wall. Living with her is going to be some party, all right.

"So," she says, turning to me with a bright smile. "Was that guy you were with your boyfriend?"

"Not yet," I say lightly. "What about you? Dating someone other than Bach?"

She bursts into giggles.

"No. I mean, there is this one guy in Virtuoso with me, but . . ." She shrugs. "He's not really worth it."

"Worth what?" I ask, surprised to find I'm actually *curious* about this frizzy-haired creature.

"Worth the distraction."

"You're awfully serious, aren't you?" I wonder if she's going to be one of those naggy, disciplined types who gets all pissy if I stay up late texting on school nights. She better not be.

"I have no choice," Nicole says with a wry smile. "If my performance slips even a little, Headmaster Higgins could pull my scholarship."

A scholarship kid. Now it all makes sense.

My phone buzzes on the bedside table, the screen flashing Mom's name. With a roll of my eyes, I pick up.

"Hey, Mom."

"Hi, mija." That's my mom's nickname for me, short for "my daughter" in Spanish. You might be fooled into thinking the nickname makes my mom the warm and fuzzy type, but no. It's what her own mother called her when she was young; I simply inherited the name, like a hand-me-down coat.

"How did today go? Your schedule looking good? Did you get into the classes we wanted?"

My mother is one of those slightly scary politico types, a fast-talker with ambition oozing from her veins. I wonder if it's her fault that the idea of being a superachiever is so unappealing to me. She makes it look exhausting.

"My schedule is fine," I tell her. "I didn't get into the APs, but whatever, I'm glad. It'll be easier this way."

I glance at Nicole, who politely turns away, riffling through her bags. On the other end of the line, I hear Mom cluck her tongue.

"That's a shame. The Ivies will expect to see some AP classes on your transcript. You'll need to work harder, Lana, and then try again for next semester."

I stay silent, waiting for her to finish her chiding.

"Just promise me you'll apply yourself, and that you won't perpetuate the stereotype of the pretty girl who falls behind academically. You know you're better than that."

I feel myself bristle at her words.

"Okay, Mom, I'll be sure not to *perpetuate* anything."

"No need to take that tone. I'm only looking out for you, mija. Now, tell me about Congressman Porter's son."

I flop back onto the bed. How am I supposed to explain to my all-business mother—especially with this new room-mate of mine listening—the feeling I got when I saw him? The one that wiped clean any sort of agenda and replaced it with unbiased desire.

"It's not a good time. I did what you asked, though." Before she can interject, I add, "Talk to you later, Mom. Tell Dad I said hi."

Nicole turns back to me as I hang up.

"What's your mom like?"

I've never been asked *that* question before. Most people know exactly who she is and what she's like.

"My mother is Congresswoman Diana Rivera, represent-ing New York," I recite. "She was elected House Majority Whip in 2014 and was recently named *Glamour* magazine's Woman of the Year. In her spare time, she and her attorney husband are spearheading the fund-raising efforts for DC's first museum of Puerto Rican Arts and Culture."

"Wow," Nicole remarks. "That was quite the official bio."

"Yeah. It's from the USA.gov website."

Nicole laughs.

"Well, she sounds incredible. You must be so proud to have a mom like that."

"Yep." And it's true, I was—right up until the moment I realized I was expected to follow in her formidable footsteps. That's when the pride grew into something else.

I'm already tired of this topic, so I turn it back to Nicole. "What about your parents?"

Her expression twists, as if she just tasted something sour.

"I don't know my dad. My mom had me pretty young, so . . . they weren't exactly a couple. But she's awesome. She just has to work a ton, being a single mom. She's an assistant to a financial adviser back home in Pittsburgh."

"Oh." I'm not sure how to respond to any of *that*. "So where did the music thing come from?"

Nicole shrugs.

"I was born with it, I guess. My dad, wherever he is, must be a musician."

I try to imagine not having a father, and the thought sends a shudder through me. My dad is pretty much my favorite thing about home.

A knock on the door interrupts us, and Stephanie waltzes in.

"Can you believe they separated us? I thought for sure this would be my room—" She notices Nicole. "Oh, hi. I'm Stephanie."

Nicole smiles shyly.

"Nicole Morgan."

Stephanie grabs my hand, pulling me toward the door.

"Come on, we're meeting Jen and Kara in the Media Room before dinner."

I wonder if proper roommate etiquette would have me inviting Nicole to come with us, and introducing her to my inner circle. But I don't. I simply give her a wave and a smile, and head out the door with Stephanie.

I can't help but feel a flicker of relief as I leave her behind.

• • •

Chace sits with the soccer team at dinner that first night, and even though we're on opposite ends of the table, I can feel his eyes intermittently flickering toward mine. I pretend to be engrossed in the chatter all around me; I smile and play along with the banter of my two closest guy friends, Brandon and Derek. But I'm just filling a spotlight.

You know how you can be part of one conversation while your ears strain to pick up another? Somehow I know Chace and his teammates are talking about me, and I crane my neck as subtly as possible, hoping to catch a snippet of their dialogue. Are they telling Chace how lucky he is to have grabbed my attention, how they've all tried and failed?

Then, out of the corner of my eye, I see that hideously un-cute pair of overalls. Nicole is approaching our table, looking like a deer in headlights as she scans the benches for an empty space. A flare of annoyance flashes through me. Doesn't she have friends and a table of her own? Is she honestly expecting us to become besties now, just because we're stuck in the same dorm?

But before she can make her way to me, Chace turns in his seat and calls out her name. I watch, transfixed, the same way other people are fascinated by the sight of car wrecks. *Why* is the most eligible guy at this school paying even a smidgen of attention to my socially and fashionably challenged roommate?

Chace starts gesturing to his teammates, making a violin motion with his hands that's rather adorable—and it hits me that he wasn't just being nice in the theater. He's actually impressed with her. Before he can invite her to sit with him, I stand up.

"Nicole!" I call out, fixing a wide smile on my face. "There you are, I was looking for you." I pat the sliver of bench space next to me, ignoring Kara's annoyed glare.

Nicole's face lights up. She gives Chace and his teammates a little wave before hurrying toward me. Chace meets my eyes, and this time I let my gaze linger. His smile is warm and admiring, as though I've just confirmed his most flattering suspicions about me. Taking Nerdy Violin Girl under my wing is just what he needed to see to prove that I'm not simply the stock pretty and popular type—that I'm actually a good person.

And right now, as Nicole plops into her seat beside me, I sort of wish it were true.

• • •

The next morning is the first official day of junior year, and it begins with a screech. I throw my pillow over my head, inwardly cussing out my roommate, who can't even manage to wait until after I'm awake to start playing her schmaltzy music.

"Sorry!" she says at the sound of my groans. "I thought I could be your slightly-more-pleasant alarm clock today."

Seriously?

"My alarm does the trick just fine," I tell her, not bothering to hide the bitchiness in my voice. She flinches, and I'd *maybe* feel bad, if it weren't for the fact that my sharp tone clearly did the trick. She puts the instrument away.

There's no hope of falling back to sleep when I'm twitchy with irritation, so I heave myself up to a sitting position and grab my phone. I find half a dozen texts from Stephanie, Kara, and Brandon—and an email from Headmaster Higgins that sends my stomach plummeting.

Hi, Lana! ☺ I hope your summer was fantastic. I'd like to set up an appointment as soon as possible to discuss some areas of concern for you this year. Can you come by my office after your last class today?

Oh, joy. Could an email scream doom and gloom any louder? Plus, who has "areas of concern" before the school year has even begun? I guess that's one domain where we can call me an overachiever.

"Are you okay?" Nicole asks, watching me.

"I'm just not a morning person," I grumble.

She takes the hint. We get dressed in our matching uniforms and pack our matching schoolbags, all without making conversation. Soon Stephanie is at the door, asking if I'll trade my Chanel sunglasses for her Burberry headband (accessories are the only personal touches allowed with our uniforms, so we have to take advantage), and as we swap the goods and head out the door, leaving Nicole to follow, I feel myself starting to relax. I'm about to be in my element. Not in the classroom, but on the social stage. I may not be a virtuoso musician, a killer athlete, or a 4.0 student, but somehow I'm the girl everyone wants to be with—or just be. I guess that's one thing I learned from my mother: how to win the popular vote.

• • •

After a jam-packed first day of rushing between new classes and catching up with all the friends I didn't have time for yesterday, I find myself at the headmaster's door, debating whether or not to blow off the appointment and pretend I never received her email. But then I see him in the waiting room.

"Hey."

Chace Porter gives me that sexy, dimpled grin of his as I walk in. "Finally a familiar face."

I settle into the seat next to him with a smile.

"I'm guessing there aren't a lot of those for you just yet?"

He chuckles. "Not exactly. I'm still getting used to everything. I owe you one, though. If you hadn't shown me that shortcut yesterday, I might have missed chemistry altogether."

"Well, hey, that wouldn't have been so bad. But I'll start thinking up ways for you to repay the favor," I say with a sideways grin.

He looks right into my eyes, his expression managing to be both teasing and intimate. And for the first time in as long as I can remember, I feel myself growing shy, looking away first.

"So." I give him a conspiratorial nudge, regaining my cool. "What are you in here for on your first day, anyway? Organized crime, weed, seduction of a teacher?"

He leans in closer.

"I have my secrets, but they're none of those."

A thrill radiates through me.

"I'm good with secrets," I tell him.

Just then, a dour-faced girl I don't recognize—must be an underclassman—walks through the door and plops into the third chair, filling our little circle and interrupting the moment. Chace leans back in his seat.

"I think Higgins just wants to get me up to speed on the curriculum and the minimum grades I have to maintain to stay on the soccer team."

"She's full of fun today," I say under my breath.

"What about you?" He raises an eyebrow. "Something tells me this isn't your first time in the headmaster's office."

I shrug modestly.

"Yeah, I've made a few appearances. I have a feeling my mom orchestrated this one, though. She's obsessed with making sure I stay on the straight and narrow and get into the right college, so she probably talked Higgins into this preemptive visit."

"Your mom sounds like my dad," Chace remarks.

"They do have a lot in common," I say. Before he can ask what I mean, Higgins's assistant is standing before us.

"Mr. Porter, the headmaster will see you now."

"Good luck," I tell him.

He's in the office for a good twenty minutes, during which time I scroll through my text messages and halfheartedly look over tonight's homework assignments. When he comes out, it's my turn.

"How'd it go?" I ask, as the headmaster's assistant escorts him to the front of the office.

He shrugs.

"No biggie. Hey, I'll wait for you if you want."

A smile escapes my lips.

"Okay."

• • •

It's just as I suspected. Mom enlisted the headmaster to give me a lecture on my subpar grades last year, and to drill into my head how crucial junior year is for me to "reverse the trend" and "step up my game" if I want to be considered by a top-tier university. Now, to put things into perspective, my GPA is a 3.5. That's on the fringes of the honor roll, for heaven's sake! It's not like I'm some D student. But, as Higgins and my mom love to remind me, a 3.5 is low for an Oyster Bay student. It's not exactly an average that will wow admissions officers from Stanford or Columbia. Forget about Harvard and Yale—I already blew my chances there, barring some miracle.

"Why do I *have* to go to one of those schools, anyway?" I ask the headmaster, though of course I already know the answer.

"Because you're an important young lady meant for great things. Your mother could wind up becoming president in the not-too-distant future, and if that happens you'll be serving as an example to girls all across the nation, not to mention representing your mother in front of the world." Headmaster Higgins shuffles some papers on her desk. "Now, something that could be of vital help is your extracurricular activities. Even the most academically competitive schools will overlook a lower GPA if someone has an extraordinary talent that would benefit their school name."

I stare blankly at the headmaster. What, does she think

my inner Lady Gaga or Serena Williams emerged out of nowhere over the summer? I think of Nicole and her violin and feel a sudden spark of anger that she doesn't have to worry about any of this.

"I've been approached by a few different modeling agencies," I tell Higgins. "Maybe—"

She shakes her head emphatically.

"That's not the kind of talent I was talking about, dear." She hands me a booklet from her stack of papers. "Here's a list of the different extracurricular activities and sports teams Oyster Bay has to offer. Sign up for a few, won't you?"

By the time I finally make it out of her office, I'm fuming. Silly me; I thought this year would be different. I thought my mom's latest lofty goals meant that she'd finally lay off me, that she'd be too busy controlling the House of Representatives to try controlling every aspect of my life. But she's still determined to turn me into her perfect image.

Chace stands when he sees me reemerge outside the office. He takes in my expression and doesn't speak until we're alone, in the relative safety of the hallway.

"You okay?"

"I have something to confess," I tell him, feeling a shot of adrenaline as I imagine how Mom would cringe if she heard what I'm about to say. "I knew who you were yesterday. My mom works with your dad at the Capitol, and she wanted—"

"She wanted you to get close to me." Chace finishes my sentence, leaning against one of the lockers in the hallway.

I stop, taken aback.

"Well. Yeah."

Chace gives me a half smile.

"My dad told me to do the same."

"Really?" Now I'm intrigued. "Why did they both . . . ?"

"Your mom is the majority whip, but my dad has the president's ear. They each want something from the other. Isn't that how Washington works?" Chace rolls his eyes, and I feel a sudden rush of affection for him. I wish it didn't have to end like this— before it even started.

"It's not only that," I admit. "I think my mom has some kind of dream of a . . . I don't know, a power alliance through us. Or something like that." My face heats up. "So were you just playing along yesterday, then?"

"At first." Chace reaches out and briefly touches my shoulder. "But my dad failed to mention how cool and un-Washington you are."

I laugh in spite of myself.

"She was cool and un-Washington. That should be my epitaph one day."

"And so pretty, it's almost blinding."

He says it under his breath, and I wonder if I misheard. But when our eyes meet, I know he meant it.

"I wonder . . ." I bite my lip, daring myself to say it. "I wonder if giving our parents what they want could be its own kind of rebellion."

"I like the way you think," he replies.

We fall back into step, and for the rest of the walk back to the dorms, we're quiet. It's as if we've said too much, and must now make up for our confessions with silence. When he drops me off at the door to the girls' dorm, he doesn't say goodbye.

"See you soon," he says instead. And I know something is beginning.

5

NICOLE

"Though time may help you forget
All that has happened before . . ."

The cop and the detective finally dismiss me after an hour of questioning, tearing open my insides and forcing me to lay myself bare as they searched the hidden corners of my heart. I know my answers left them dissatisfied; I saw the frustration written in their eyes every time I had to say the words *I don't remember* or *I don't know.* But at last they let me go, handing over their business cards and urging me to call if I think of anything that could help the case.

"We'll be in touch," Detective Kimble says, patting my arm as she walks me to the door. I hope she's wrong about that. I hope I never have to see either of their faces again.

I manage to keep it together as I shuffle out of the headmaster's office and back into the hallway. My eyes remain trained on the carpeted floor, my head down, trying to block the sound of my classmates' grief from my ears. I keep it all in, holding my breath, as I step outside and cross the quad.

Then I'm running.

The tears lodged in my throat break free and I can't see where I'm going, the moisture blurs my vision. But I know where I'm headed. My body shudders with sobs and I crumple to the ground, gripping fistfuls of grass and dirt.

"Whenever I'm alone with you,
You make me feel like I am home again."

His warm voice fills my mind, singing a song that once was ours. I look up wildly, half expecting to see him standing before me, extending a hand to help me up as he tells me about the elaborate prank he pulled. But I'm all alone, lying in the field of dandelions beneath the wooden bridge—the place we used to call our little sliver of heaven.

"Whenever I'm alone with you,
You make me feel like I am whole again,"

I whisper back.

There's no answer, of course. I lie back against the grass, curling into the fetal position, and close my eyes. Maybe if I stay like this, if I don't move . . . it will all go away.

. . .

"Nicole. *Nicole.*"

I blink back into consciousness. A boy's tall shadowy frame stands above me, his head bowed as he watches me with a frown. It's Ryan Wyatt, Chace's roommate and closest friend at Oyster Bay.

Chace. The horror of it all comes flooding back and I sit up quickly, the blood rushing to my head.

"Did—did—" My throat is like sandpaper. "Did you hear?"

Ryan kneels down to my level. The broken expression on his face tells me everything I need to know.

"He's gone," I whisper. My throat closes up around the words, I'm struggling to breathe. Ryan grips my shoulders.

"Nicole, you can't fall apart," he warns me, but the ragged edge to his voice lets me know he's been crying, too. "You've got to keep it together. Do it for Chace."

I shake my head violently.

"Why? He's—he's—"

"Then do it for you," Ryan says more sharply. "The cops are in my room right now, digging into everything of Chace's—his phone, computer, all of it. That means they're going to find out about you guys. You've got to get your head straight."

I fall back against the grass, spreading my arms like some sad snow angel.

"You're too late. They already questioned me."

Ryan was always the nicest out of Chace's friends. Or maybe I should clarify: he's the only one who actually acknowledged me. In those brief, heady days when I thought we were going to be together, Chace confided in Ryan about us. To my surprise, Ryan didn't immediately assume it was a joke, or tell Chace he'd be crazy to give up Lana's exotic beauty for the plainness of me. He actually seemed to . . . get it. And after my accident, he was one of the very few who didn't cringe when he came face to face with me and my scar.

"How did you know I'd be here?" I ask Ryan now.

He lowers his eyes.

"Chace told me this was where—"

I nod quickly to stop him from talking. We remain in silence for who knows how long, me lying on the grass with my face tilted up to the cloudy sky, a numb, drugged feeling washing over me, while Ryan sits upright, hugging his arms to his chest.

"I should go home," I finally say. "Back to Pittsburgh, I mean. I have to get out of here."

"You can't," Ryan says heavily. "There's Chace's funeral to figure out, and—"

"As if Lana would ever dream of letting me be involved," I cut him off.

"You still have to be there," Ryan insists. And he's right. Even though it might kill me, I know he's right.

"After the funeral, then." I turn onto my side.

"You don't get it, Nicole." Ryan looks at me seriously.

"You can't go anywhere until the cops figure out what happened. You're a person of interest now."

Person of interest. Of course, I sensed that's what I was from the moment the detective and the cop started grilling me, but the idea is too ludicrous, too unfair, to be spoken aloud.

"Why are you even here?" I snap. "What do you want, anyway?"

"I'm here because I know how Chace felt," Ryan says. "So I can only imagine how you feel right now."

An invisible fist takes my heart and twists it, the words *too late, too late* taunting in my ear. I was too late to realize he still cared for me, too proud to ask or give us another chance. The photo in his pocket, his best friend's words, they are proof of my irreparable mistake.

"I spoke to Chace's parents." Ryan's voice is barely above a whisper. A terrible shiver runs through me at the thought of what they're facing. "They're flying in from Washington tonight. There's going to be a candlelight vigil."

Stop talking. Please stop.

As if he can read my thoughts, Ryan gets to his feet. "I'll leave you alone. I just needed to—to be around someone who understood."

I should go with him; I should comfort him. Doesn't the best friend have more of a right to grief than the illicit non-girlfriend? Doesn't he deserve to have me asking what I can do to help *him*, letting him cry on my shoulder?

I'd like to think I will, and soon. But not yet. I need to

stay out here, alone in our special place, for as long as I can—before the world rushes in to disturb it.

. . .

I lie there past sunset and into the darkening night, staring up at the changing sky. Could he be up there already, one of the stars gazing down from above? Or is he still here, mingling with the air and the wind surrounding me?

My hands are twitching, unaccustomed to going this many hours without playing the violin. It will be a relief to have the Maggini cradled in my arms again, to exhaust my pain into the music, and practice until my muscles ache and my fingers bruise.

Lights flicker in the distance. I hear a pack of footsteps, followed by the sound of mournful singing.

> *"Well, I've heard there was a secret chord*
> *That David played and it pleased the Lord . . ."*

I recognize the voice. It's Mandy Taylor, a choral student from the Virtuoso Program. I've accompanied her a dozen times before, but tonight she sings alone.

I pick myself up off the grass and cross the little wooden bridge, leaving our special place to follow the singing. This must be the candlelight vigil Ryan told me about. While I couldn't imagine attending before and sharing my grief with all of them, I'm now frantic at the thought of missing it.

Mandy's voice, intermingled with the sound of marching footsteps, leads me to the southernmost lawn behind the school. I fall into step with my classmates at the entrance to the soccer field, blending into the crowd. They are a blur of stricken faces and dark clothing, of shaky hands clutching candles and waving signs reading WE LOVE YOU, CHACE and CHACE PORTER, FOREVER IN OUR HEARTS. The sight sends dread churning through my insides all over again.

I spot Brianne trailing behind our orchestra group, her face pale in the glow of candlelight, but I duck before she can see me. I don't have it in me to make conversation, to explain where I've been.

As we file through the open fence onto the field, I'm caught in a flood of memories. I haven't been back here since junior year, and a montage of happier times plays in my mind—sitting in the stands with Lana, cheering whenever Chace scored a goal, the three of us plus Ryan goofing off when the field was ours after practice, and later . . . waiting for Chace alone, catching his eye and watching him smile just for me.

Mandy's singing stops, and I'm yanked out of my reverie by another familiar voice. Lana steps up onto the stands, a microphone in her grasp.

"Today we lost one of the best guys we'll ever know," she says, her voice catching on the words. "From the moment Chace arrived at our school, he brought with him an energy you couldn't help wanting to be around. He was the greatest friend to all of you, and the best boyfriend to me."

Is it my imagination, or does Lana find me in the crowd just then, giving me a pointed stare?

"He was an amazing teammate, big brother, and son. And—" She swallows hard, and through the candlelight I can see the torment on her face, belying her composure. "We owe it to Chace to do everything we can to help the police find the monster who did this to him."

This time I know I'm not imagining things. Lana is definitely eyeing me, her mouth curling in distaste. But she can't think—

The sound of car tires roaring onto the field startles me out of my thoughts. My classmates turn to look, murmuring to each other. Headmaster Higgins is going to have a conniption over this. The Oyster Bay grounds are strictly car-free zones. But then I take in the black limousine, and I understand. Lana drops the microphone into someone's palm and starts running toward the limo.

The uniformed driver jumps out and hurries to open the rear doors. Mrs. Porter steps out first, unrecognizable from her polished press photos. Her face has a deadened expression, her body hunched over as if carrying the entire weight of the tragedy on her back. The congressman steps out next, his mouth set in a grim line. Twelve-year-old Teddy follows, taking his mother's hand. The scene is too much to bear, and I turn away, a searing pain blazing in my chest.

But out of the corner of my eye I can see Lana rushing toward them, wrapping Mrs. Porter in a tight hug. Ryan threads through the crowd of classmates to join them, embracing the congressman and crouching down to talk to Teddy.

No one wants me here. And if I thought or hoped that I might feel Chace with me at this moment . . . I was wrong.

I make my way through the throng and off the field, keeping my eyes on the ground so I won't have to witness one more sight that breaks my heart.

You'd be surprised at how challenging it is to pull off a decent party at boarding school. With nothing but a corridor to separate the girls' wing from the boys', Oyster Bay Prep *could* be a breeding ground for all sorts of deliciously fun shenanigans—but the constant supervision they keep us under nipped that prospect in the bud a long time ago. So when our astronomy teacher, Mrs. Wakely, announces that a midnight meteor shower will be lighting up the sky on Friday, I'm gifted with a momentary flash of genius: What if we threw a school-sanctioned Meteor Shower Bash (aka coed outdoor slumber party) to take advantage of the last blush of summer while doing something kind of academic?

"I mean, doesn't it sound incredible? We can take turns looking through the telescope and then sketch what we see by the light of bonfires. We can stargaze and roast marshmallows," I urge Mrs. Wakely after class. "And instead of just going back to our dorms after the meteor shower and forgetting the whole thing, we can fall asleep in our tents beneath all the action in the sky. What do you think?"

In case you're wondering, no, I'm not some kind of astronomy fanatic. The first two weeks of classes and the accompanying boatloads of homework have me itching to shed my buttoned-up school uniform, to dance barefoot and sneak sips from a flask, to flirt with Chace Porter and let him see others flirt with me. But I manage to convince Mrs. Wakely that my interest in this whole idea has nothing to do with the social perks.

It's hard for people to refuse me, even teachers, and Mrs. Wakely is quickly swept up in my enthusiasm and making arrangements with Headmaster Higgins. After that I'm the hero of the day, getting high fives in the hallways and whispers in my ear of "I'll sneak the vodka." Mrs. Wakely will be chaperoning, which might have been a wet blanket on the night if I hadn't remembered a key detail. *"I could sleep through a tornado,"* she once said mournfully, when recounting to the class a comet that blazed across the sky in the 2000s—something everyone in her life managed to stay awake to witness but her. I'm banking on history repeating itself, and Mrs. Wakely being a fabulously *unobservant* chaperone.

Part of the deal was that I'd be in charge of setup, but I don't even mind. I enlist Stephanie, Derek, and Brandon for the morning of the party, and of course Nicole offers to help as soon as she hears what we're up to, so I have four other sets of hands pitching tents and stringing lights from the trees on the South Lawn. When Stephanie asks Nicole who she's "tenting with," I feel a momentary pang of worry that I'm expected to invite her to share our tent. I mean, don't I deserve *one* night off from making small talk with this girl I have nothing in common with? Thankfully, Nicole replies that she's sharing with Brianne and another chick from orchestra. It's a relief to know she has actual friends besides that violin of hers.

Friday night approaches, and dinner flashes by in an excited blur. Soon it's time for Mrs. Wakely to lead our class out of the dining room, past the envious stares of the seniors, who never had the sense to come up with an idea like this when *they* took Astronomy. Moments later, we're outside and hiking toward the South Lawn, adjacent to the soccer field. It looks like a summer dream after our decoration job.

Twinkling lights and paper lanterns hang from the trees, patio chairs fill the spaces between tents, and a large patch of grass is kept clear for dancing. Three tables stand together on the outskirts of the tents, holding pitchers of ice water and lemonade, dessert platters, portable speakers, and, to placate our teacher, astronomy cards. From our classmates' whoops as they enter, it's clear that this outdoor slumber party I dreamed up is a winner.

Stephanie cues up the playlist, and our favorite Rihanna track starts blaring. She shimmies over to me, and before Mrs. Wakely knows what hit her, the sedate little astronomy gathering I promised her turns into a dance-off. I bump hips with Stephanie, let Derek twirl me around, and then I dance alone in the center of a growing crowd, lifting my arms above my head and showing off my toned abs as I do my best Shakira moves. I scan the faces cheering me on, and my eyes find Chace's. Knowing he's watching sends a thrill tickling down my spine. I look away, pretending I didn't see him—but he's the one I'm dancing for.

After starting with such a bang, I'm thrown when the rest of the night doesn't go according to plan. I don't know what I expected exactly, but it definitely *wasn't* watching as my crush got chatted up by every other girl in our class. Two hours and three drinks later (yes, we spiked the lemonade, duh) he still hasn't even approached me. Of course, it only makes me hunger for him more. So I do what any girl in my position should. I laugh harder and louder than everyone else. I dance with whichever guy bops over to me, regardless of whether or not I find them repulsive. I keep that "Happiest Girl in America" smile fixed on my face, ignoring Chace as steadfastly as he appears to be ignoring me. But when my eyes flick back over to him and find him deep in conversation with *Nicole*, of all people, I feel my energy deflate. Why is he wasting time with all these other jokers, when I'm practically offering myself up on a silver platter?

After half an hour of pretending to pay attention to my friends' chatter while secretly watching Chace and Nicole out of the corner of my eye, I finally stalk past the two of them, heading for the telescope. I don't give a hoot about what's going on in the sky, but at least it gives me something to do while I formulate my next move.

I'm squinting into the lens, trying to figure out what's so thrilling up there, when I feel a hand on my shoulder.

"Hey," Chace says, his breath warm against my neck. "What's up?"

"Hey," I reply, still looking into the telescope. I'm not about to turn around and drop everything just because he *finally* decided to pay attention to me.

"Something tells me Mrs. Wakely is going to pull the plug on the music soon," he says into my ear. "Want to get a dance in before she does?"

Based on the panicked expression I saw on our teacher's face while watching a group of us grind our hips and shimmy our shoulders to "Bitch Better Have My Money," I have a feeling Chace might be right. But still. I'm not about to give him the satisfaction of a dance so easily.

"I'm a little busy right now," I tell him, nodding at the telescope.

"Is anything happening up there yet?" he asks.

"I can't tell," I admit grudgingly.

He laughs, a warm and wonderful sound, and leans in so his shoulder is touching mine.

"Let me look."

"So what were you and my roomie talking about?"

The words just slip out, and my cheeks blaze in embarrassment. *Why* did I say that aloud? It must be because I'm just so baffled that he even has two words to say to her. They couldn't be more different.

"We were talking about you, actually."

Now I can't even feign indifference. I step away from the telescope, eyeing him.

"Really?"

"Yeah." He gives me a teasing grin. "I think she might be hatching some sort of plan. Like trying to set us up."

"Oh?" My heartbeat picks up speed. *What is Nicole doing?*

Chace turns to face me, neither of us bothering with the telescope anymore.

"She asked me if I'm too chicken to ask you to dance, and if it's because you look so good tonight."

"She did *not* say that." I let out a nervous giggle.

"Did too."

"So what did you say, then?" I'm fishing, I know, but I can't help it.

Chace looks at me thoughtfully.

"I asked her what you're really like. And she said you're as nice and as cool as you are pretty."

For the first time in my entire life, I'm stumped for words. First of all, let's be real, even *I* know I'm not as nice as I am pretty. But more importantly, why would Nicole do this for me? I've hardly been buddy-buddy with her since we became roommates—our interactions have mainly consisted of her making small talk and me muttering in reply—so she was clearly stretching the truth with her compliment. Why would she say it? What does she have to gain from me landing my crush?

"Come on." Chace reaches out his hand. "I love this song."

He leads the way to the makeshift dance floor and wraps his arms around my waist. A flock of butterflies sets off in my stomach, which feels so weird. What *is* it about this guy that makes me nervous when I'm normally so self-assured?

> *"You know the night's magic seems to whisper*
> *and hush . . ."*

He hums along as I drape my arms around his neck, and I can't help relaxing into a laugh.

"What is this song? Did Mrs. Wakely switch to her own old-person playlist or something?"

"That's an intriguing thought." Chace pulls me in for a playful spin. "But if you don't know who Van Morrison is, then I've got some educating to do."

"Okay. Just as long as I get to do some educating of my own." I look pointedly down at my feet, which he's now stepped on twice. We both laugh, and he draws me in closer.

My arms are tingling. Something electric is in the air. I can't keep up my hard shell in his embrace; I'm turning soft and mushy inside, like those girls I always made fun of. I feel myself becoming one of them now, melting into a romantic. Maybe I should try to fight it, but I don't.

It feels too good.

It's five in the morning and I'm lying awake in the tent, too giddy to sleep, listening to Kara's snores. The girl really needs to start taking a decongestant stat. If it were yesterday, I might have shaken her awake and snapped at her to shut up, but I'm feeling particularly gracious at the moment.

He likes me. It's such a middle-school phrase, yet it has the power to set off a small fireworks explosion in my chest. *He likes me.*

A shadow approaches the tent and I sit up, curious as to who else would be awake at this ungodly hour. Then I see the outline of frizzy hair as she passes. I quickly climb out of my sleeping bag, throw on a sweater, and crawl out of the tent.

"Nicole," I call out in a stage whisper.

She whirls around, her eyes wide.

"You scared me," she says with a giggle. "I thought no one was up. I can't sleep."

"Me neither," I tell her. "Where were you going?"

"Just for a walk. I thought the post-meteor-shower sky would be something to see. I feel like I missed the main event last night."

"Me too. I don't know if Mrs. Wakely built up the whole thing, or if we're all blind as bats."

We fall into step together, passing the tents and moving onto the soccer field.

"Nicole? Why did you say those nice things about me to Chace?" I blurt out.

Two pink spots appear in her cheeks.

"Because I knew you liked him. I could tell from the first time I asked you about him. And I don't know, he was talking to me and I guess . . . I just thought I should give him a little push."

"So you wanted to help get us together? But why?" I'm still trying to process the idea of someone doing something for me without an ulterior motive.

Nicole gives me a quizzical look.

"Because I know you like him, and you're my friend. I just thought it was right."

Her simple words leave me speechless for the second time in twenty-four hours. Here I've been complaining about this girl behind her back for two weeks, and meanwhile she thinks we're *friends*. She wanted to do something nice for me and she did. She gave him a push.

"Thank you," I finally say. "You're a good friend."

And in that moment I decide I'll be a real friend to her, too.

"Look!" Nicole cries, pointing upward. "Finally!"

A spark races through the sky, followed by another and then another, like multiplying bolts of lightning.

"There it is." I look up at the sight of the meteor shower making its appearance at last. The sparks accelerate into a celestial rainfall, shooting closer, and I take a nervous step back.

"Don't worry," Nicole says with a smile, slinging her arm across my shoulder. "They're only stars."

7

NICOLE

OCTOBER 24, 2016

"But, honey, it's too late to regret
What is gone will be no more."

Instead of taking the direct route to my dorm, something pulls me toward the South Lawn. I'm close enough to hear the mourners, to see the flickering candles from their vigil, but now I can breathe my own air.

I turn slowly in the empty green space. If I close my eyes, I can see it as it looked that night last year, with the tents and the paper lanterns, Lana and her friends tearing up the patch of grass that passed for a dance floor. It's hard to imagine that one meaningless party could alter the course of our lives, but it's true. Everything stems from the decision I made that night.

What if I'd made a different choice? The thought has haunted me for a year. What if I'd recognized Chace's interest those first weeks of school, instead of finding it so unfathomable and pushing him toward Lana instead? In my mind, guys like him belonged with girls like her. I wanted to see them together, my stupid ego needed to prove my insecurities right. And yes, I wanted to be her friend, too. Those months of staying up late talking and sharing secrets like sisters, of being included in her innermost circle—they almost made my decision worth it.

Some friends we turned out to be.

With a shiver, I turn away from the lawn and the ghosts of last year, picking up the pace as I make my way back toward the dorms. But it isn't long before the ghosts find me again.

The wooden bridge is the midway point between the school's sprawling fields and its main buildings. Underneath the bridge, in my and Chace's sanctuary, you can't see the forest it leads to. But from above, passing the bridge means I'm forced to see the moss-covered trees, their branches stretching toward me like mangled fingers, beckoning me back inside. I'll never make that mistake again. But even without going near it, the forest still swallows me up in flashes of memory.

"Lana?" I repeat as I move through the woods, struggling to keep my balance on the craggy path. "Where are you guys?"

My palms grow clammy as I realize I really ought to be hearing the sounds of the party by now—but there's nothing. No music, laughter, or clinking bottles, only the occasional hoot of an owl.

I fish my phone out of my pocket, but the No Service warning flashes at the top of the screen. Shoot.

I hear a flapping sound behind me and I cry out, whirling around in panic, but it's only a harmless bird. Holding my flashlight in front of me like a weapon, I notice a sheet of paper taped to the tree in front of me. The words "Party Up Ahead!" are scrawled in Lana's handwriting, above an arrow pointing north. I release the breath I've been holding and continue along the trail.

But even as I keep walking, I'm no closer to the action. The woods are still dead silent, with no sign of anyone here but me. When I reach the low cliff that splits my path in two, a sick realization dawns on me.

I shake my head violently to rid myself of the memory. I can't bear to relive that night—even though I'm forced to face its aftermath whenever I look in the mirror.

• • •

I step back into my dorm for the first time since this morning, before my world was shattered. It feels like someone else's space now. My phone, plugged into the charger in the wall, beeps and flashes and I can only imagine how many messages are waiting for me. I have a brief fantasy of shoving my phone in the sink and letting it die, but then I imagine my mom's panicked face. She's probably been trying to reach me all day. There's no way the news hasn't gotten out yet—not when it's the congressman's son.

I reach for my phone tentatively, as though it could

burn my fingers. I have nine missed calls—five from Mom, one from Ryan, another from Brianne, and two from unfamiliar numbers that give me a sinking feeling. What if it's the cop or the detective with more questions I can't bear to answer?

My text message inbox is flooded with the same names, and multiple variations of *Are you okay? I'm worried, call me!* from Mom and *Where are you?* from Brianne. I start to type a reply to Mom, but I can't get past the word *Sorry* before my throat tightens and tears burn my eyes. I hurl my phone across the room, watching as it skids over the carpet and hits the leg of my desk. There's only one person I want to speak to, whose name I ache to see in my message inbox. And I never will again. The thought is too much to stomach, and I grab my earbuds and iPod off my bedside table, desperate to drown out the noise in my head. I scroll down to a Brahms playlist and slip the buds into my ears.

> *"However far away, I will always love you.*
> *However long I stay—"*

My heart leaps into my throat. I sit upright, giving my iPod a double take, but the screen still shows *Brahms: The Symphonies* as Now Playing—even though the Cure's "Lovesong" is the melody filling my ears. Our song.

And then I hear something else. His voice over my shoulder, singing along quietly, just like he used to. I rip off the earbuds and whirl around, holding my breath. *Could it possibly be—?*

Of course not. The room is as empty as it was when I walked in. I sink back onto the bed, weakened with disappointment.

Yet I could swear I still hear him humming.

OCTOBER 25, 2016

I wake up with my phone in my hand, waiting for a text that will never come. I don't even remember falling asleep. I'm still wearing yesterday's school uniform, and my contact lenses feel like glue in my eyes from sleeping in them.

"Nicole!" There's a pounding at my door. It's Brianne, her voice sounding flustered.

As I heave myself up to a sitting position, the horror of yesterday comes rushing back to me all at once. I cry out, gripping the bed frame. No, it wasn't a nightmare. It's a new reality I'll be forced to get used to, morning after morning.

"Nicole, let me in!"

I push myself off the bed and make my way to the door, still in a daze. But when I open it, I'm in for a shock. Brianne isn't alone. A crowd of girls is clustered in the hallway behind her, all of them watching me like I'm some kind of main attraction, their eyes probing and hawklike. Two of Lana's minions, Kara and Jen, are among them, their arms folded aggressively as they stare me down. *What the hell?* I close the space in the doorway so that only Brianne can slip inside. She pushes past the voyeurs and slams the door behind her, then leans against it, catching her breath.

"What's going on? What are they doing out there?" I ask her.

"Sit down," she orders.

I sink back onto the bed, staring at my friend in confusion. She grabs my laptop off the desk, types something into the search window, and then thrusts it in my lap. I take one look at the screen—and my heart stops. I jump up in panic, letting the laptop crash to my feet. *No, no, no.*

It's our photos. They're on the front page of Google News, underneath the boldfaced headline, "The Case of Chace Porter and the Girl in the Picture." I stare at the article in disbelief as the room begins to spin.

Someone got their hands on our photo strip—and now anyone and everyone can see me sitting in Chace's lap, his lips on my shoulder. It's all there, in permanent color ink.

"How did this happen?" I whisper. It hurts to see the photos again and remember what I've lost—as if I could forget—but it's even harder to wrap my mind around the loss of our private moment, the broadcasting of our secret. My mind flashes through a series of imagined reactions to the pictures: my mom's shock, his parents' confusion and pain, Lana's fury. *She's going to kill me over this,* I realize, and then it hits me that it's no exaggeration. *She might actually kill me.*

"Exactly. How did *this* happen?" Brianne gestures at the fallen laptop. "You guys were going out behind her back? How could you lie to me for so long? You always acted like you barely knew him, and now this. . . ." She trails off, shaking her head in disbelief.

I ignore her questions. I don't know what I can possibly say so that she'll understand. "How did these get out?" I ask instead.

"I don't know, but they're everywhere," Brianne warns me. "TMZ broke the story and it took off from there."

I try to breathe, bending over and lowering my head to my knees.

"Nicole." Brianne's tone softens slightly. "What happened?"

"It was messed up," I say under my breath, avoiding eye contact. "That's why I didn't tell you, or anyone else."

"I thought you and Lana were friends," she says, giving me a funny look. "Did you forget those months last year when I barely saw you outside orchestra, since you were so busy with Lana and her group? Why would you do this to her?" Brianne's eyes harden with recognition. "I guess now I know why you came running back to us."

I flinch.

"It's not what you think. I'm sorry, I never meant—" I close my eyes, take a deep breath, try to explain. "We fell in love. It was real, the kind of thing you can't fight. It's just that simple. There wasn't anything malicious about it." The words sound familiar as they come out of my mouth, like a rehearsed speech, and then I remember: this is exactly how we put it to Lana, before the end of junior year. Tears well in my eyes, and I cover my face with my palms.

Brianne pats my shoulder awkwardly. I can tell she's trying to be there for me, but she's beyond thrown by all of this. She doesn't recognize her friend anymore.

"But, Nicole . . . if it's what you're saying, if it *was* real love, then why were you sneaking around behind Lana's back? Why didn't you just tell her the truth instead of—instead of him cheating on her?"

"We did," I whisper. "It wasn't cheating. We were going to be together, but—but then—" I gesture to my face.

"The accident," she breathes. Her eyes flash and suddenly she's indignant on my behalf, instead of at me. "Don't tell me he dumped you because of the scar?"

"No, but it . . . it changed everything." I look away. "It felt like my punishment. And then when we could finally openly be together, imagining all those eyes on me and my face—I just couldn't do it. Everything happened so quickly. It was too much."

Brianne stares at me, eyes wide.

"Oh, Nicole. I wish you had told me all this before."

"I know. I do, too. But . . . well, remember when you and JJ split up?"

Brianne stiffens at her ex's name. They were camp counselors together, and she used to ecstatically mark off the days

74

till summer by drawing big red hearts on her calendar. But that all stopped last fall.

"Obviously I remember. What about it?"

"You went from talking about him all the time freshman and sophomore year to not even mentioning his name anymore once you guys broke up. You didn't even really tell me why you broke up," I point out. "So we're similar in that way. People like you and me, we don't talk about our pain. We play it. We throw it all into our music instead of putting it into words."

Brianne looks at me uneasily.

"I still say this is different—"

She stops midsentence as the sounds from the hallway grow louder, turning into a chorus of hisses coming at me from behind the closed door. I can make out two words: *"Scarface"* and *"Slut."* Scar-faced slut. I feel like I'm going to be sick.

"I can't stay here," I tell Brianne.

She nods quickly.

"You should ask Higgins if you can take a leave of absence and go stay with your mom. I'm sure she'll say yes."

"But—but then I'd miss the Orchestra Showcase." The thought is almost as terrible as staying here with the hissing at my back.

"It might be smart to stay offstage until this dies down, honestly," Brianne says.

I know she's right, but the thought twists my insides. If Chace is gone, and I can't perform, then what do I have left?

"I guess I'll just . . . just hide out in here until Higgins gives me the okay to go home." I scuff my toe against the carpet. "What do you think I should do about Lana? I mean, we don't talk anymore, but . . . part of me feels like I should say something about the pictures—"

Brianne cuts me off, shaking her head emphatically.

"Nothing you say will do any good at this point. If you want my advice, it's to do what you probably should have done last year: stay away from Lana Rivera."

• • •

I spend the rest of the dreary day locked in my dorm, sitting on the floor with my back against the bed, hugging my knees to my chest. It seems I'm incapable of anything else. I don't even have the stomach for the lunch Brianne smuggled through my door, not with the catcalls and hissing continuing unabated. It seems that every time one set of mean girls has to abandon their post outside my door to attend to their actual lives, another group takes their place. I'm dying to get out of here, but Headmaster Higgins still hasn't responded to my email. And even when she does, that won't stop the attacks online.

I finally call my mom back, and she's every bit as hysterical as I expected.

"What in the world, Nicole? I couldn't reach you all day, and suddenly your friend is dead and your picture is in the paper—" She bursts into tears.

"It'll be okay, Mom," I say automatically, but of course that's an outright lie. "I'm going to try to come home."

I hear her take a big gulp of air.

"But your scholarship—"

"Only for a little bit, until things . . . settle down. And only if the headmaster says it's okay." I glance at my locked door. Higgins will probably be glad to see the back of me, with all the distraction I'm causing.

"I'm going to talk to my boss, see if he has any lawyer recommendations."

My blood turns cold.

"A lawyer? Why?"

Mom sighs heavily.

"Honey, the things they're saying in the paper . . . and the boy's parents are so powerful . . . I just want you to be protected."

"So we had a relationship. How could anyone think that makes me a criminal?" I stare at my phone, aghast.

"I'm just trying to cover all our bases," she says, attempting to sound reassuring. "They tend to look at the victim's significant other first in these types of cases."

"Then they should focus on Lana," I say darkly.

The moment we hang up, my phone is back to vibrating again. This time it's from Facebook, alerting me to all the new messages and posts on my page. With a sinking feeling in my stomach, I log in.

Backstabbing, boyfriend-stealing, scar-faced slut, reads the first from Katie Minor, a girl in my Algebra II class. *Did you kill him too?!* reads another, from someone whose name I don't recognize but whose profile picture is of a wholesome-looking woman cradling a baby. On and on the hateful and gossipy messages continue, attached to different names and different smiley profile photos that belie the cruelty underneath. My heart is palpitating in my chest, and I scroll up to Settings. Delete Account, it tempts me.

Yes, please.

Deleted. With that, I toss my phone across the room and bury my head in my hands.

"Play."

My head whips up. What was that?

"It'll make you feel better," I hear him whisper. "Even if for just a little while."

Goose bumps rise on my arms and I feel myself shiver, even as the room grows strangely warm.

"Chace?" I blurt out, my voice wobbling. "Is that . . . you?"

"The song you were playing when we met." His voice seems to come from everywhere and nowhere all at once, echoing across my dorm room walls. "Play that one. It'll quiet them all."

My whole body trembles. I want nothing more than for this to be real, but how can it be? I'm obviously hearing things, or having some kind of post-traumatic hallucination. Still, I get up and unpack my Maggini, following the illusion even if only to give myself something to do. I cradle the violin under my chin, position my hand on the bow. And as I play "The Immigrant Theme," I feel something new, something almost supernatural, coursing through my veins, dripping from my hands into the music. When I finish the song, my body slowly coming back down to earth, I realize he was right.

My playing really did shut everyone up.

• • •

Just before six, the hour when I'd ordinarily be going down to dinner, I hear footsteps approaching my door.

"Nicole," a female voice calls out—a voice that is decidedly not Brianne's. "It's Detective Kimble and Officer Ladge."

My stomach plummets. I make my way to the door, keeping my eyes on the ground to avoid the stares of the stragglers who have nothing better to do than spy on my bedroom door. I've changed out of my uniform by now and am wearing a pair of flannel pajamas, which makes the scene inside my pocket-sized dorm room even weirder—me, a cop, and a detective filling the cramped space between my bed and dresser.

"How did the pictures get out?" I demand as soon as Detective Kimble closes the door behind her. I don't mean to sound so accusatory, I know I should be on my best behavior in front of them. But I can't help it.

"I'm afraid there was a breach," Officer Ladge says mildly, as if it's some unimportant, routine occurrence. "We'll get to the bottom of it."

"But—but that *shouldn't* have happened," I sputter. "Those pictures were private, and now—now I can't even leave my room!"

"Unfortunately, the photos ceased to be private the moment they were found on the body of a murder victim," Detective Kimble says. "We hoped to keep this under the radar, too, but with all the news coverage on the case, it would have gotten out eventually."

"We're installing extra security at the school in light of all the attention the case is getting, and we'll make sure to have your door manned at all times so you can feel safe." Officer Ladge actually has the nerve to smile at me, as though *this* is going to make everything better.

"Thanks, but I'm actually going to go stay with my mom for a little while," I tell him. "Hopefully by the time I come back—"

"That won't be possible," Kimble interrupts.

I'm sensing a pattern here. She's obviously taken on the Bad Cop role, while Ladge pretends to be Mr. Nice(r) Guy.

"I've spoken to your headmaster," she continues. "We need you to stay put until the investigation concludes."

"What? *Why?*" I swallow hard. "I'm not in any trouble, am I?"

"No—" Officer Ladge starts to assure me, but Detective Kimble interrupts.

"Not yet. But it's our job to investigate everyone closest to the victim, so we'll need to keep you nearby for any further questioning. And as Officer Ladge said, we'll assign you a security detail so that you can come and go to your classes safely."

I slump into my desk chair, leaning my head against my knees.

"Is that what you came to tell me?"

"Actually, no." Kimble pulls a laminated paper out of her coat pocket. "We have a warrant to search your room."

"*What?*" I cry. Fear jolts through me as I spin around to take in my former haven of a bedroom, filled with my most precious music, my secret writings, mementos and photographs from before the accident. They can't go through my things, they *can't*.

"It's all very routine," Officer Ladge says in his attempt at reassurance. "We've done the same with the victim's room, and a couple others. There could be important pieces of information in your possession that you're not even aware of."

I watch in panic as Detective Kimble pulls a plastic bag out of her briefcase and she and Officer Ladge slip on latex gloves. What the hell are they expecting to find in here? I keep my eyes on the floor so I won't see them empty my desk, rifle through my chest of drawers, and examine the bottles of pain medication and tubes of scar cream lining my sink. But I can hear it all. And at the sound of arms lifting my violin case, I jump back to my feet.

"Not that! You can't take the Maggini. She's all I have."

"We're just looking," Kimble says. I hold my breath as

she opens the case and runs her unworthy fingers across the instrument, feeling underneath for something, anything, that could pass as evidence. But of course she finds nothing, and I'm able to exhale again as soon as she puts the Maggini back in its case. But now, glancing around my room, I see they've half emptied it. Framed photos, journals, my laptop—they've all been dumped into Kimble's bag. They even had the nerve to go through my *trash*. Rage rises up inside me.

"When will you give everything back?"

"As soon as we've cleared it all for any important evidence," Officer Ladge replies. "We'll supply you a temporary replacement laptop for your schoolwork, or anything else you need." Again with that smug smile, as though I should be thanking him for ransacking my room.

"One last thing," Detective Kimble adds. "The victim's parents have, of course, seen the photos. They want to speak with you."

My head jerks up.

"His parents? When?"

"Tomorrow. We've arranged a meeting for you after class."

8

LANA

Chace takes hold of my hand as we step into Le Rocquefort, the restaurant his parents chose for our first meeting. It's the kind of fancy-schmancy place my own mom and dad would be at home in, complete with white tablecloths, Christofle silver, and menus with no prices listed. I'm no stranger to this kind of scene. I spent the bulk of my childhood tagging along with my parents to upper-crust establishments, surrounded by people three times my age. But tonight is different.

After almost two months of dating—including one month Facebook-official—I'm meeting Congressman and Mrs. Porter, and I've never cared more to be liked. Making a good impression is easy; I can do that with my eyes closed.

But being actually *liked* and embraced by his family? That's a different story.

"There they are." Chace gestures to a corner booth.

I smooth down the sides of my skirt as we approach, my heartbeat picking up speed. It took me forever to choose an outfit for tonight, but I finally settled on a Chanel shift dress, a birthday gift from Mom. Even fashion-clueless Nicole agreed it was perfect. She was practically giddy as she ushered me out the door, telling me how gorgeous I looked. Let's hope the Porters will feel the same; that they'll rave about me as soon as I leave the room, just like Chace's teammates do.

"Mom, Dad!"

Chace hugs them both, granting me a split second to study the Porters before it's my turn to be on display. The congressman is taller in person than he appears on TV, with salt-and-pepper-streaked hair and sharp features set off by blue-gray eyes just like his son's. His voice is deep as he greets us, his presence powerful. Mrs. Porter, on the other hand, seems a bit . . . well, mousy, if I'm being honest. She's pretty enough for her age, with glossy brown hair and a very Kate Middleton–style coatdress. But she hangs back from her husband, her voice timid. Let's just say she's the polar opposite of my mother—which means I'll probably adore her.

"You guys, this is the girl I've been telling you about. Lana Rivera."

I step forward with my most winning smile, extending a hand.

"It's a pleasure to meet you, Congressman and Mrs. Porter."

"And you as well." Congressman Porter shakes my hand with vigor. "I work with your mother at the Capitol, so I've been hearing about 'the beautiful Lana' from more than just my son."

A happy flush heats my cheeks. So far, so good.

The waiter hurries to our table to pull out our chairs and we take our seats, with me seated between the two Porter men.

"So, how did you two meet?" Mrs. Porter asks, as the busboy fills our water glasses.

Chace grins at me.

"Lana was the Good Samaritan who took pity on me my first day. She showed me the ins and outs of Oyster Bay, and after that I kept noticing her everywhere I looked. Everything seemed a little brighter when she was around."

My stomach gives a thrilling swoop at his words. It feels like every day I'm discovering new things to love about him, including what a romantic he is for a guy our age.

"Isn't that sweet?" Mrs. Porter turns to her husband with a smile.

"Very." Congressman Porter eyes me over the top of his menu. "So, did you two know of your political connection when you first met?"

"That our parents work together, you mean? Yes, we knew. The real surprise was that it didn't deter us," I say with a laugh.

"And what does Congresswoman Rivera have to say about it?" he asks with a slight smirk.

"Um, she's happy, of course."

"Really?" His eyebrow arches.

I look from Chace to his father. Am I missing something here? Why does he look so smug when asking about my mom? But just then the waiter appears at my elbow.

"Are you fine folks ready to order?"

We haven't even opened our menus, but Congressman Porter starts rattling off a list of selections for the table, from foie gras starters to the Wagyu beef with pommes frites, and chocolate ganache "drizzled" with gold shavings for dessert. Someone apparently isn't too concerned about the bill.

"So, tell us about yourself, Lana," Mrs. Porter says in her soft voice, after her husband finishes ordering half the menu.

"Well." I pause, contemplating the question I've been asked a zillion times and still loathe. "I spent my childhood in Manhattan, before my mom was elected and we moved to DC. I'm an only child, since my parents' dual careers didn't leave them much time for kids. But it's never bothered me because I have a ton of friends who are like family, anyway." *What else?* "Oh, and I love fashion and traveling. My grandparents live in San Juan, Puerto Rico, so we spend the first two weeks of summer vacation there every year."

"Lana is an awesome dancer, too," Chace adds.

Mrs. Porter lights up.

"Are you in Oyster Bay's dance program? Ballet or modern?"

I laugh awkwardly.

"No, Chace was just flattering me. I like to dance for fun, that's all."

"Oh, isn't that nice."

I sense a tinge of disappointment, and my newfound insecurity flares up. What if she wanted someone more accomplished for her son? My own mother's words echo in my ears: *"In the upper echelons of DC society, it's not enough to simply be beautiful and popular. You've got to have something more, Lana."*

Right. So . . . what is my "something more"?

Our first courses arrive and soon we're busy digging in, with the Porters making conversation about their holiday plans, Chace's soccer career, and how his younger brother, Teddy, is doing at his new middle school. I chime in wherever I can, doing all the little things that usually make me the life of the party—displaying my signature wit, smiling like a girl with the world at her feet, pretending I'm having more fun than anyone else. And then a moment arrives where I spot an opportunity to score some points.

"Seriously, though," I say, while we're on the subject of Chace's recent winning game. "As if it's not impressive enough that he's a total star on the field, he also happens to be the nicest, humblest guy I've ever met. Let me guess—he's probably never given you a day of trouble in your lives, am I right?"

It's meant to be a butter-'em-up compliment, of course. The Porters should smile magnanimously, tell me how great it is to see their son with a girl "who clearly *gets* it."

But instead, Mrs. Porter drops her fork with a clatter, and the three of them exchange a look.

"We got lucky, I suppose," Congressman Porter finally says, smiling like the politician he is. But I know politicians, and I can tell he's hiding something. What could it be? I turn to Chace, but he's not looking at me. His eyes are focused on the table.

After the moment of awkwardness, Congressman Porter starts in on a series of questions about our teachers and classes, and soon the dinner returns to normal. But in the back of my mind, I can't stop wondering . . . what was it about my remark that triggered such a weird reaction?

• • •

Chace's roommate, Ryan, is out on a date of his own, so we find their dorm blissfully empty when we get back from dinner. I'm crossing my fingers for Ryan to score tonight, more for our sakes than for his. After two months of dating, Chace and I are still at a very PG-level of hookups, thanks to the utter lack of privacy here at Oyster Bay. I'm dying to sleep in the same bed, to curl my body into his, to run my lips over every curve.

"Lana?"

Chace repeats my name, looking at me questioningly, and my cheeks heat up. I wonder if he can guess where my mind ran off to.

"Sorry, what did you say?"

"I was just asking if my parents were what you expected. If they're like yours." He sits on the bed and pulls me onto his lap.

"Well . . ." It's hard for me to focus with his hands around my waist. "I guess so. Your dad and my mom have the same sort of steeliness about them. Your mom was really sweet." I pause. "Why did everyone act funny when I said you must have given them no trouble? I was only talking up my man." I give him a teasing look.

Chace tightens his grip around me.

"Eh, I wasn't always the best kid."

I look at him dubiously.

"Well, I can't imagine you ever being a bad boy. I mean, you actually *like* Nicole's classical music. That has to make you a bit square, sorry to say." I laugh, but Chace doesn't seem to get the joke.

"Some people are bad by accident," he says simply. "Or they're forced into it."

"Okay, well, now you've got me intrigued." I give him a light poke in the ribs. "Spill."

A shadow crosses his face, and then it's gone as quickly as it appeared. His expression lightens, and he pulls me down onto the bed with him.

"It was just your run-of-the-mill immature drama, nothing even worth talking about." His hands move up my back. "I'm much more interested in *you* right now."

My thoughts disappear as our lips meet. Everything drops

away; nothing matters but the boy in my arms. Who would have thought it was possible to feel this way?

"I like you a lot, Chace Porter," I whisper between kisses.

He smiles back at me, his gaze genuine.

"I like you for real, Lana Rivera."

• • •

I make it back to my dorm at close to two in the morning, after Ryan's return forced me and Chace to say a reluctant good night. I tiptoe across the corridor to the girls' side, mentally rehearsing my excuse in case the dorm warden catches me ("I lost my favorite bracelet and was just retracing my steps!"), but luckily I make it to our room unseen. I'm expecting to find it dark and silent, but Nicole is awake, sitting up in bed staring at a piece of paper. She perks up when she sees me.

"Hi! How did it go? You're home late, so that must be a good sign."

I drop my purse and jump onto my bed with a happy sigh.

"It was magical. I mean, being alone with Chace after dinner was. His parents were . . . okay."

"Just okay?" Nicole asks.

I shrug.

"A little weird and cagey. I couldn't tell if they liked me, to be honest."

"Well, it's impossible that they didn't," Nicole says confidently, and I feel a rush of affection for my unlikely new friend.

"What's that?" I nod at the paper in her hand.

"Oh." Nicole's face floods with emotion. "It's from the New York Philharmonic. They chose me as violinist for their Contemporary Orchestra Youth Showcase this spring." She shakes her head in amazement. "They chose *me*."

"Oh my God!" I lean across the bed to give her a hug. "Congratulations. You so deserve it."

For the briefest second I wonder what it might be like to be her, to be the very *best* at something and have your future all mapped out. But then, of course, I wouldn't get to be me. And I wouldn't be the girl Chace likes.

"We should celebrate," I tell Nicole. "Before we leave for winter break tomorrow, let's go to that dessert-only place. You, me, and Chace."

Nicole's cheeks redden.

"Oh, you guys probably don't want me tagging along on your date."

"No, you dork, we're going to be celebrating you!"

"Well, if you're sure. That's nice of you." She smiles, but I notice a cloud behind her eyes.

"What is it? Why aren't you freaking out with excitement right now?" I ask.

She smiles sheepishly.

"I am freaking out, I just . . ." She sighs. "Brianne and I practiced so hard for the audition together. I guess I always pictured it happening for the two of us."

"Ah. So she didn't get in."

Nicole nods, biting her lip.

"She left me a voice mail in tears. Apparently her cello spot went to some guy from LaGuardia. I haven't called her back. . . . I don't know how to tell her I got in."

"You just have to rip off the Band-Aid and do it," I advise her. "It's like when the guy Kara was into asked me out last year. It sucked having to tell her, but she got over it."

"Yeah, it's just that Brianne is really intense about things. Everyone in the Virtuoso Program kind of is," Nicole says. "And she's having such a rough year so far, what with the breakup with JJ and all."

"Okay, Nicole. You know I love you, but enough about Brianne." I flop dramatically on the bed, and she laughs. "We have way more exciting things to talk about."

"You're right," she says. "I'm just being overly sensitive about it. Tell me more about your date."

I smile into my pillow and begin recapping the entire electrifying night.

9

NICOLE

It's all your fault.

I can't sleep, my mind ticking a million miles a minute as I stare at the text message from Lana. She sent it hours ago, right after Officer Ladge and Detective Kimble left my room carting a bag full of my personal belongings with them. My iPhone confirms what I already know—that this is the first real contact I've had from Lana in five months. I thought she deleted my number, erased every trace of me from her life. I guess I was wrong.

The message just above this one, all the way back to May 26, bears three telling words. *Go. To. Hell.* But the previous texts from Lana Rivera might have been written by a different person altogether.

Hey girl, everyone's coming to our room for *The Bachelor* tonight, XOXO!

This is a text from May 10, while the messages farther up in the chat window are sprinkled with emojis, inside jokes, and plans to meet here or go there. Scrolling through the texts is like picking at a bloody scab, feeling the pain all over again of a friendship lost. It seems impossible that these two girls no longer speak, that *"XOXO"* so quickly devolved into *"Go to hell."* But maybe she is right—that it is all my fault.

I type, delete, and re-type my reply, unable to find the right words. Finally I settle on the most banal possible response.

What do you mean?

So far she hasn't replied, but I already know her answer. *"If you hadn't gotten involved with Chace, he would still be alive."* I can't tell if the voice in my head whispering these words belongs to Lana or me. But either way, somehow I know it's the truth.

I throw the covers off me and swing my legs over the bed. There's no hope of sleep tonight. My room, once the only place where I felt safe at Oyster Bay, is contaminated now, infected by Officer Ladge and Detective Kimble's presence. It doesn't even feel like mine anymore, not with the journals missing from my desk and photos stripped off my wall.

I glance at my bedside alarm clock, which reads 2:30 a.m. If there's ever going to be a safe time for me to escape my room and breathe the outdoor air without getting harassed, it's now.

After changing out of my pajamas and into a pair of jeans and a sweatshirt, I grab a flashlight from under the bed and slip into a pair of flats. I'm not sure where I'm going—only that I need to get out of here.

Sneaking out in the middle of the night is a run-of-the-mill thrill for most Oyster Bay girls, something that lost its fear factor once they realized they could actually get away with it. But tonight is my first time breaking the rules, and my heart is hammering so loudly in my chest, I'm half convinced it'll give me away. I can just *see* the triumphant expressions on Detective Kimble and Officer Ladge's faces if they catch me running through the grounds, searching for a hideaway. *"Now* do you have anything you'd like to tell us?" I imagine Kimble saying smugly, with that suspicious look in her eyes. The thought is nearly enough to send me tiptoeing back up to my room but I press forward instead, following the marble staircase down to the lobby of the Dorm Wing. But on the second landing, I hear a low, frenzied din of voices coming from the Dining Hall—and my stomach jolts. I'm not the only one awake.

I wager a quick debate in my mind. Do I dare stay and find out what sort of clandestine meeting is taking place in the middle of the night? Or should I make a beeline back to my room before I get caught? The latter is clearly the wiser choice—but then I hear a cool female voice say, "My concern is for Lana, of course." And I find myself inching forward, switching off the flashlight so I can blend into the dark, feeling my way along the walls until I reach the closed door to the dining hall.

A man inside mumbles something too quiet for me to hear, even as I press my ear against the door. And then a familiar voice cuts through the others. It's Headmaster Higgins.

"What do you expect me to do?" she asks.

"Make a statement saying what a devoted girlfriend Lana Rivera was, and what a model student and citizen she still is," comes a voice that I now recognize as belonging to Lana's mother. "Tell the press that she is in no way a suspect."

My heart leaps into my throat. Lana . . . a suspect?

"That's the police's call to make, not mine," I hear the headmaster say stiffly. "I don't doubt that Miss Rivera had nothing to do with it, but I'm not convinced of your theories surrounding Miss Morgan, either. And clearly the police are just as skeptical, or they would have brought her into custody."

"It's only a matter of time," Mrs. Rivera says smoothly. "I understand she's under investigation."

The sound of my name, mixed in with all the ugliness spoken behind these closed doors, is like a punch to the gut. I cover my mouth with my palm, biting back a cry. She's setting me up, then. Lana and her mother are trying to make *me* look like the culprit—but for what? Revenge for loving Chace? Still, it makes no sense that Chace's parents would entertain any of this, much less in a shady, under-the-table meeting.

As if hearing my thoughts, another woman speaks up. This must be Chace's mother.

"It's not right," she says, her voice shaking with rage. "My son *died,* and not even forty-eight hours later the two of you are making this about politics and appearances? It's repulsive."

A chair pushes back with an angry screech, and I plant myself against the wall, terrified that she's about to storm out and discover me eavesdropping. But then the man speaks.

"I hate this just as much as you do, but we have no choice. We have to protect ourselves. We have to protect Teddy." After a pause, he says, "Please, sweetheart."

Protect themselves? From what? Haven't they already lost what matters most?

My head is spinning, and it seems the narrow hallway is growing ever tighter, making it a challenge to breathe. The dark engulfs me like quicksand and I feel myself sinking into it, falling into the words and plans of the adults plotting in the next room. Until I'm shaken out of my trance by the sound of whistling coming from the other end of the hall.

It's our song, once again. Only this time, I can't let the sound of him slip away. I follow its echo blindly, all thoughts of Chace's parents and Lana's cold mother slipping from my mind.

"However long I stay, I will always love you."

I whisper the lyrics like an incantation as I chase the sound that seems to be one step ahead of me. I wind my way through corridors and run down the stairs, following the whistling until I'm throwing open the doors of the dorm wing and standing outside in the quad, shivering underneath the night sky.

At first, all I see is the ordinary Oyster Bay landscape of Gothic campus buildings and vast lawns, darkened by night's paintbrush. But then the whistling starts up again— and a figure floats past me, his feet skimming just above the ground.

"Chace!" I try to scream. But no sound comes out. In my shock, I'm only capable of mouthing his name.

I whip around wildly, my eyes searching for him—or whatever it was I saw. And then I glimpse a luminescent shadow standing on the front steps of Joyce Hall. I watch, my whole body prickling in astonishment, as the shadow fills with color, forming the image of the boy I loved. The boy I *love.*

It takes my body a few moments to recover and remember how to move. But when it does, I run faster than I ever have before, sprinting toward him even as my hateful mind taunts me, telling me I'm imagining things, that of course this can't be real.

"*Chace.*"

This time, I manage to speak. I'm standing before him now, separated by only two steps, waiting for him to turn around. And then he does, and I sink to my knees.

I must be dreaming, but I don't care. All I know is that I'm looking up into those blue-gray eyes, which are alight with emotion as they gaze down at me. His mouth opens to speak, and I reach out my hand to touch his cheek. He immediately shakes his head, sadness darkening his features. I draw my hand back, somehow understanding that I can't touch him anymore.

"I shouldn't be here," he says. His voice sounds different, muffled, as though he's already far away. "I should go, but I can't—I can't leave you. I don't want to make the same mistake twice."

"Come back," I plead, my throat thick with tears. "Please. Don't leave me again."

"Even letting you see me is breaking the rules," he whispers. "But I had to."

"I don't understand any of this." My voice breaks and I move closer, until there's only a sliver of charged space between us. "What happened to you, Chace? *How* did this happen?"

He looks away, turning his face up to the moon.

"Do you remember how we—we fell in love?"

"Of course I do. I remember every detail."

"The answer is in those days." He turns back to meet my gaze, jarring me with his determined expression. "I'm trying to remember the last moments before everything went black, but that's all that keeps coming to me. You and me. Last spring. The answer is there."

My insides turn cold.

"What? Do you mean it's my fault that you're . . . ?"

"No, I mean something happened when we were together that we need to remember." He closes his eyes, as if in pain. "It's just so hard for me to remember things now."

I ache to wrap my arms around him, but I'm afraid to. Afraid my hands will brush against emptiness instead of flesh and bone, proving that this is nothing more than a vision.

"Was it—was it Lana?" I ask. It seems crazy, but her mother's words are still ringing in my ears. If she was worried about her own daughter, then maybe there's something to it.

"I don't think so," Chace says. "Lana might be responsible for a lot, but she's not a killer."

I release the breath I've been holding. I didn't want to believe it, either. But then . . . who?

Suddenly, Chace's skin takes on an otherworldly glow. He stares at his palms, panicked.

"I have to go."

"No, wait!" I beg. "Chace, they—they're trying to make it seem like I did it. Please don't leave me."

But his image is already fading in front of me.

"If anyone can uncover the truth, it's you. Remember the days of you and me. The answer is there, I can feel it."

And with that, he vanishes before my eyes, leaving me to wonder, through tears, if I imagined the whole thing.

OCTOBER 26, 2016

My new life of security guards and lawyers begins the next morning, with my mother showing up at my door. I've never been so relieved to see her, and as I fling myself into her arms, I don't even notice the strangers.

"Oh, sweetie," she murmurs, smoothing back my unkempt hair and taking in my appearance. My pale skin and undereye circles from lack of sleep only enhance my scar, making me look even more frightening than usual. If Mrs. Rivera and the police are trying to turn me into the villain, I certainly look the part.

"What are you doing here?" I ask my mom, pulling her through the doorway. "I didn't know you were coming—"

My eyes lock on a burly man posted by my door, wearing a bored expression and a SECURITY badge. So this must be who Detective Kimble and Officer Ladge were talking about yesterday. He seems effective enough already—yesterday's gaggle of girls are now gone.

But he's not the only stranger. Another man, this one

much more polished and wearing a suit and tie, follows my mom into the room uninvited.

"'Scuse me, who are you?" I ask, giving Mom a bewildered look.

"Sorry, honey, I should have introduced you." She steps between me and the suited man. "This is attorney John Sanford. I know him from the office, and he's agreed to represent you pro bono, thank God for his kindness."

A chill runs through me.

"A lawyer? Already? I'm not in trouble." *Yet.*

John Sanford steps forward, shaking my hand.

"At this point, since you're a person of interest in the Chace Porter case, I'm afraid you need legal counsel immediately. I understand you've already spoken to the police?"

I nod.

"They searched my room, too." At the look of alarm on my mother's and the lawyer's faces, I quickly add, "They had a warrant."

Mr. Sanford rubs his chin, thinking.

"What time is your first class, Nicole?"

"It's at eight-thirty, but . . . am I really going?" The idea of sitting in a classroom seems ludicrous at a time like this.

"You have a Juilliard scholarship to maintain," Mom warns me. "You can't afford to let anything throw you off your game. Not even this."

After my visit—or vision—from Chace last night, everything else pales in comparison. Juilliard, my music, all my old dreams feel like they belong to someone else. Is there even a point to it all anymore?

As if she can read my thoughts, Mom grabs my shoulders, gazing into my eyes.

"Nicole, this is what you love, what you breathe. You've been working all these years to get here. One day, impossible as it may seem right now, you *will* recover from all that's happening, but you may never get over the regret if you choose to let your dream slip through your fingers. Trust me on this. I had to struggle my way through adulthood, but you don't. Not with a talent like yours."

My eyes find my violin case across the room, and the pang in my chest confirms my mother's words. Of course she's right. The world can take nearly everything away from me—my face, my friends, my love—but as long as I have my music, I have something worth living and fighting for. I have a purpose.

"Okay," I finally reply. "I'll go to my classes. But it's not going to be pretty."

Mom squeezes my hand.

"I'm proud of you, honey. We'll get through this together."

"Your mother is right. And the more normal your day-to-day life can be, the less suspicious things will look," Mr. Sanford adds.

My cheeks burn.

"There's nothing *suspicious* going on."

"I understand. But when you're hiding out in your dorm

and skipping classes, it could look like you have something to hide," he says pointedly. "Now, I suggest the three of us get out of these tight quarters and find a place to get breakfast before your first class. You can fill me in on your conversations with the police there."

"I should probably tell you something before we go." I swallow hard. "Chace's parents asked Detective Kimble to arrange a meeting with me today. I'm supposed to meet them after my classes are over."

Mom and Mr. Sanford exchange a worried look.

"Right. Well, there's no way you're doing that alone," Mr. Sanford says.

"What if they just want to meet the girl who was . . . who meant something to their son?" I ask hopefully, though after what I overheard last night, I'm not so sure. "Wouldn't it look weird for me to bring a chaperone if that's all it is?"

He gives me a grim smile that doesn't reach his eyes.

"Nicole, I'm afraid from here on out, you're going to have to assume that no one's intentions are that innocent. The congressman and his wife are grieving parents who need someone to blame. You can't be too careful."

10

LANA

DECEMBER 31, 2015

Nicole, Stephanie, and I stretch our legs across the leather banquettes on the mezzanine landing of my family's DC town house, watching the preparations taking place in the foyer below for tonight's New Year's Eve party. Uniformed men are rolling up carpets, pushing back furniture, and assembling round tables and banquet chairs, while a small army of florists darts around in different directions, arranging table centerpieces and draping garlands from the twin Baccarat chandeliers dangling from the ceiling.

I've always relished these frenzied hours before a party kickoff, from the hustle and bustle of the staff downstairs, to the cool elegance of my mom applying her makeup in a cloud of perfume up in the master suite. The anticipation gets me every time, the promise of some sort of magic to come, as our house is transformed into a wonderland. And tonight, my excitement is more warranted than ever: Chace and his parents are coming to the party. The thought of my boyfriend here in the house where I grew up, looking movie-star gorgeous in his formal wear and dancing with me in front of all of DC's high society, gives me a palpable thrill.

Our longtime housekeeper, Gabby, whose gray-streaked hair is beginning to show her age, approaches with a fruit and cheese platter.

"Here you go, girls."

"Oh, thank God. I'm starving," Stephanie says dramatically, breaking off a hunk of Gouda with her fingers. I can't help making a face at Nicole. I love Steph and all, but the girl needs to learn how to use a cheese knife.

Nicole isn't looking at me, though. She's staring at Gabby, color filling her cheeks.

"What's up?" I elbow her in the ribs.

"Did I ever tell you my mom worked as a housekeeper when I was little?" she blurts out, after Gabby steps away.

Stephanie's eyebrows shoot up. I clear my throat.

"Uh, no. That must have been . . ." My voice trails off. What's the appropriate response, anyway? *God, that must have been weird!* doesn't exactly have the best ring to it.

Nicole shrugs.

"It's not that big of a deal, I guess. She ended up going

back to school and now she works in an office, but even if she hadn't moved on, I know there's obviously nothing wrong with being part of a household staff. It's just . . . well, I never really pictured her in that role until now. The family she worked for had teenagers, too, and it just seems strange, the idea of her waiting on kids our age when she had a little girl at home." She glances at me. "Does your housekeeper have children?"

I don't think I've ever exchanged this many words about Gabby in my life. What is Nicole getting at? Stephanie lets out a yawn, clearly bored with this conversation.

"Um, I don't know," I answer. "Maybe?"

A crash sounds from downstairs. The three of us turn to look over the railing, where the head florist is cursing out one of her underlings, who frantically sweeps up shards of a dropped vase.

Nicole looks away, cringing. I suddenly see this whole scene from her point of view, and the glamour of it all is replaced with . . . something else. But why should I feel guilty or have to apologize for the pomp and luxury that surrounds me? My parents earned this. Maybe Nicole sees her mom's face when she looks at Gabby or the staff downstairs, but that's her problem. Not mine. Right?

"I'll be right back," I tell the girls, getting up from the leather seat. I need to restore my balance, and watching my mom beautify herself, in her cloud of Chanel No. 5 should do just the trick.

• • •

My parents' master bedroom is practically the same size as the Oyster Bay football field. As a little girl I managed to get lost in it once or twice, but now there's something comforting about the airy space, with its sleek slate-and-cream furniture, weird modern art, and Baccarat crystal adorning every shelf.

I find my mom in the adjoining marble-floored bathroom, perched on a director's chair and jabbing at her phone while Pierre, the family hairdresser, blows out her silky dark strands. She looks up at the sound of my approach and smiles into the mirror.

"There you are, mija. I thought maybe you'd grown out of watching the regimen this year."

"Nope." I pause to air-kiss Pierre before settling into the love seat next to Mom's vanity table. "What dress did you choose?"

"The red McQueen," she replies. "Which calls for a red lip, of course. Why don't you wear your Christmas present, the silver Balmain? So our colors will complement each other."

"Perfect," I agree, tucking my legs underneath me while watching Pierre's wizardry with the blow dryer.

Sometimes it feels like these are the only times I can relax around my mother. Up here, surrounded by hair tools and makeup and fabric swatches, I can pretend that we're much more similar. I can forget, even if only for a few moments, how terrifyingly serious and whip-smart she is—and how neither of those traits passed down to me.

"Pierre, do you have time to do the girls' hair when you're done with mine?" she asks now.

"Really?" I sit up straighter. Mom has only lent her hairdresser to me once, on the occasion of my sweet sixteen.

"Certainly I have time, madame," Pierre replies.

"That Nicole could certainly use your help," Mom says with a chuckle, patting Pierre's hand.

"But please don't do anything too drastic," I tell him. "I don't want to be the clichéd popular girl who gives her nerdy friend a makeover. We've only seen *that* in a million movies."

He nods in agreement.

"As you wish. No cliché hair here."

A few minutes later Pierre finishes my mom's style, giving her glossy waves that fall over her shoulder, a flawless contrast to her usual tight updos at the Capitol.

"It looks perfect, Pierre," she says, giving the mirror a satisfied smile. "Why don't you start with Stephanie or Nicole downstairs so I can have a few minutes with Lana."

Once we're alone, she looks at me expectantly.

"So? How are things going with Chace? You haven't told me much."

My stomach flutters, as it's been doing lately every time I hear his name.

"He's . . . everything I wanted. He's not only the most handsome guy I know, but on top of that he's sweet and funny, and he understands me better than most people because his parents are so similar to you and Dad. And I can't even tell you how good it feels to walk around school on his arm."

"I'm so glad, mija. See?" She arches an eyebrow at me. "Mother does know best!"

"In this case, at least." I laugh.

"Now, there's something I need you to do for me. And it involves Chace." She takes my hand, caressing it like she used to do when I was a little girl, her little doll. "It's come to my attention that Congressman and Mrs. Porter share an unreported bank account—and they've been using it to funnel a couple hundred thousand dollars to a private address in Brooklyn. Have you heard Chace mention anything about people they know in Brooklyn?"

I stare at my mom, my stomach churning with nausea as it dawns on me what she's saying. And here I thought she actually wanted a little mother-daughter bonding.

"No, he hasn't said a thing. What are you doing, Mom? Why would you be digging into their private business, anyway?"

"I work for the president of the United States," she counters. As if I actually need reminding. "If I discover something fishy involving someone on our council, it's my job to look into it and make sure the president is protected."

I give my mom a sideways glance. I'm pretty sure she just inflated her job description.

"I thought you're supposed to serve New York constituents. What does that have to do with filling the president in on the Porters' finances?"

"I don't like your tone, Lana," she says warningly.

"And I don't like what you're asking of me!" I retort. "I thought you *wanted* us together."

"I simply want to make sure the Porters are who they say they are. That's all." Mom purses her lips. "Especially with their son dating my only daughter."

"Again, what *you* wanted," I snap. "And I'm actually happy, so please don't screw this up for me."

Mom sighs.

"Enough with the dramatics, mija. I'll leave you and Chace out of it. His parents are coming tonight, anyway. I suppose I can warn them privately that the information has gotten out and see what they say. They might have a reasonable explanation for it all." She fixes her best politician smile on her face. "I'll give them the benefit of the doubt."

•   •   •

The three of us weave through the crowd of beautifully dressed guests, looking for a familiar face. It's already ten p.m. and there's still no sign of the Porters. I refuse to lose my cool in front of Stephanie and Nicole, but my anxiety bubbles under the surface. I don't have any messages from him on my phone . . . is it possible he's standing me up? Could my mom have managed to get to his parents and wreak her havoc already?

"Don't worry, Lana," Nicole murmurs into my ear. "He'll be here."

"Of course he will. I'm not worried."

I flash her a confident smile, and for a second I'm taken aback by how more-than-decent she looks in her blue sleeveless dress paired with the silver Kate Spade cardigan I gave her for Christmas, identical to the one of mine she always complimented me on. Pierre kept his promise not to give her a teen-movie makeover, but with her sandy-blond hair blown out instead of in its usual mass of frizzy curls, she looks . . . good. Cute, even.

"Oh, there he is!" Stephanie points to the doorway. It takes all my willpower not to run straight into his arms, and instead wait coolly for him to come to me. He is achingly handsome in his suit, breaking into a grin as he meets my eyes across the throng.

"Hey, babe." He sweeps me into his arms and kisses my cheek. Relief floods through me.

Chace turns to Nicole, and does a double take.

"Nicole. Hey." He gives her a warm hug, and for a split second I wonder if I should be worried. But duh, that's ridiculous. He greets Stephanie with a hug, too, and the four of us make our way to the patio.

"This is some crowd," he remarks once we're outside and able to hear each other.

"That's my parents for you. Speaking of, where are yours?"

Chace glances down.

"There was a situation with my grandmother. They're with her now."

"Oh, I hope she's okay." I take his hand. "It's so sweet of you to still come."

He smiles at me.

"I wasn't going to bail on you."

"Aww, you guys are soo cuuuute," Stephanie drawls, and Nicole giggles. I nuzzle closer to Chace.

The music pauses inside, and I see my parents making their way to the staircase, drawing everyone's attention in all their power-couple couture glory.

"Welcome, everyone, or as we say here at home, bienvenidos!" Dad raises his champagne flute to the crowd, and a chorus of clinking glasses follows. "Dinner is served!"

"Looks like I got here at the perfect time," Chace remarks.

We follow the crowd to the buffet, where platters are heaped high with surf and turf, two different salads, and an array of sides. Just as we're heading to one of the round tables decorating the foyer, Mom appears alongside our group. I feel myself stiffen.

"You must be Chace!" She extends a diamond-adorned hand to my boyfriend, who quickly turns to greet her.

"Thanks for having me, Congresswoman Rivera. My parents send their apologies. I was just telling Lana they had an incident come up with my grandmother that they had to take care of."

Mom masks her disappointment well, but I feel a flicker of glee that she didn't get her way this time. At least for one more night, she won't be able to pry into the Porters' business.

"Oh, that's a shame," Mom purrs. "I hope your grandmother's all right. I'll have to call and check in tomorrow."

To my surprise, my mom then turns to Nicole.

"Nicole, dear, Lana tells me you're quite the star violinist. What are the chances you'd play a little something for the crowd during dinner? We're giving the deejay a break, and instrumental is more appropriate for dinner, anyway, don't you think?"

Nicole's cheeks flame red. I feel a surge of mortification.

"*Mom*, don't you see her plate? We were just about to eat."

"After you're done, of course," Mom says breezily.

"That's okay," Nicole says. "I get too nervous to eat before any sort of performance. I can just play something now, if you'd like."

"You don't have to," Chace says to Nicole under his breath. I can tell he didn't mean for us to hear, but my mom's sharp expression lets me know that she did.

"It's okay," she murmurs to Chace. "They've been so nice to me."

For some reason I can't understand, it hurts to see Chace being protective of my friend. I mean, he's probably just being nice to her *because* she's my friend. But then it hits me. In this moment, he's more concerned about her than he is about me and my mom. Even though I agree that Mom shouldn't be treating Nicole like a hired entertainer, still, what right does he have to intervene?

"You guys can have mine," she says, handing her dinner plate to Stephanie. "I'll be right back."

"Come on," I tell Chace and Stephanie, after Nicole goes

upstairs to get her violin and my mom leaves in triumph. "Let's go find seats."

• • •

"I have a little surprise," Mom announces, once the guests are all seated at the round tables dotting the foyer, forks and knives poised to dig in to dinner. "My daughter's friend and roommate from Oyster Bay Prep School is treating us to some live music tonight. Take it away, Nicole!"

Nicole follows my mom to the front of the room, her expression verging on panic as she looks out at all the expectant faces. Homegirl might be used to performing, but clearly she's rattled by having to put on an impromptu show for half of Congress.

"Um." She swallows hard. "Happy New Year, everyone." And then she begins to play.

I'm used to hearing Nicole practice what she calls "scales" in our dorm room, playing the same annoying sequence of notes over and over until I want to hit her with my pillow. I'm not used to . . . *this*. I'm not used to music that pierces my insides, that covers my skin with goose bumps, that makes me want to cry for no reason.

I glance at Chace. He's watching in openmouthed amazement, as if she's the only thing that exists in this moment. But he's not the only one. Looking around the room, I see all of my mom's jaded colleagues and friends rapt, their forks frozen in midair, forgetting to eat. An older man dabs his eyes with a handkerchief.

That's my friend up there, I remind myself. I'm proud of her, I am. But I also feel a red-hot, searing envy. What have I ever done in comparison? I've never been able to bring a room to an awed hush. My parents have never looked on proudly as my talents moved people to tears. I might be a star in my little world at Oyster Bay Prep, but Nicole is an *actual* star. And the way my boyfriend is looking and listening to her right now, it makes me feel . . . insignificant. Something I never imagined I could be.

Nicole finishes the song with one final, breathtaking note. And then, after a moment of silence, the foyer fills with applause. The applause grows to a standing ovation, and of course I rise to my feet alongside Chace and Stephanie.

"How's *that* for proving Oyster Bay is teaching our students well?" my mom exclaims as she rejoins Nicole, giddy from her idea proving such a success. She hugs my friend and iPhone flashes go off, her guests capturing the moment. And I'm happy for her, I am, I am. I'm not jealous.

I'm not jealous.

11

NICOLE

I follow Mom and our new lawyer down the path to the school gates, my face shadowed by a baseball cap and sunglasses. I have to admit, as terrified as I am of the outside world right now, it does feel good to get out of my claustrophobic dorm room. But as we get closer to the gates, Mr. Sanford suddenly stops, wincing at something up ahead. I follow his gaze to a throng of spectators outside the campus gates.

There must be fifty or more people standing there, their heads peeking through the iron railings, their cameras *snap snap snap*ping. I must have turned numb, because it takes me a full moment to remember that the spectators and cameramen are all here because of what happened to Chace. And because of me. I turn away as fast as I can, before any of those people can realize they've found me.

"Scratch my earlier plan," Mr. Sanford says. "I'll pick up some breakfast for us at Starbucks and bring it back here. We'll just have to find a somewhat private place to talk."

"The theater is almost always empty at this hour," I tell him. "We can meet you there."

I regret my idea as soon as Mom and I push through the doors into Joyce Hall. What was I *thinking*, bringing this trauma into my favorite place? This is the room where I experienced some of my happiest, proudest moments; this is the stage where I first played for Chace. And now it's tarnished, just like when Detective Kimble and Officer Ladge infected my room.

"I can't," I tell Mom, shaking my head violently. "I can't do this here. Let's just talk in the lobby or something. I don't care who sees us."

Mom knows better than to argue with me. She brushes her hand against my cheek.

"Sweetie, what was the song that made you want to be a musician?"

I give her a funny look.

"You know my answer by heart. What does that have to do with anything, anyway?"

"It has to do with reminding yourself of who you are whenever life threatens to push you down," Mom says intently. "You're still Nicole Morgan, the most amazing, talented, beautiful person I know."

Tears well up in my eyes.

"Can I possibly still be her, after everything that's happened?"

Mom takes my hand with a nod.

"Tell me the song. What was it again?"

I wipe my eyes with the back of my hand, remembering what I told Chace ages ago, at the Riveras' New Year's Eve party, when he asked me what I had just played.

"It's Gershwin's 'Summertime.' That's the song that made me fall in love with music. The first time I heard it, I was so young, and it was so beautiful, I wanted to crawl inside the notes and live there among them."

Mom smiles.

"See? You're still you."

• • •

I find Brianne waiting for me on the front steps of Academics Hall as I make my way to class, escorted by one of the dozen new security guards employed by Oyster Bay Prep. She rushes over to give me a hug, and I'm relieved to see that her shock and hurt over my secret seems to have worn off.

"How are you doing?" she asks, her eyes flickering between me and the other students filling the quad, all of them turning to stare at us as they pass.

"Um . . ." I swallow hard. "I guess I'm doing about how you'd expect."

She squeezes my shoulder.

"Well, it's super brave of you to go to class."

"I don't know about brave. I didn't really have a choice," I admit. "Mom said if I get any sort of truancy record, that would mess with my Juilliard scholarship."

Brianne nods, lowering her gaze, and I immediately regret bringing up the J-word. She doesn't have a verbal commitment from the president of the music program there, like I do. She has the upcoming audition hanging over her head instead.

"Come on." I take her arm and we follow the rush of students inside the building, the silent giant of a security guard tailing us. People stop in their tracks and whisper as we walk past, but I manage to keep my eyes trained above their heads.

"Nicole, Brianne. How are you holding up?"

I turn, startled to hear a friendly voice in these halls. It's Ryan, wearing a black ribbon tied to his shirt pocket. *For Chace,* I realize, my stomach twisting.

"I miss him."

I didn't expect to blurt it out, least of all with a security guard hovering over my shoulder. But it's the truest thing I could have said.

"I do, too. It still doesn't seem real." Ryan falls into step with us. "I can't stand to be in our room anymore."

I look at Ryan, noticing the dark circles under his eyes, and I feel a pang in my chest.

"I'm sorry, Ryan. That has to be brutal."

He nods, eyes on the ground.

"Did you hear about the—the weapon?"

"What?" I stop in my tracks. Brianne shoots me an alarmed glance.

Ryan lets out a slow exhale.

"So you didn't know. I guess I shouldn't have mentioned it. It's just been all over the news for the past couple hours."

"I've been avoiding the news." I swallow hard. "What . . . what was it?"

"A kitchen knife," he says quietly. "They're saying it must have been swiped from the party."

The hall sways. Brianne grabs hold of my arm, keeping me upright.

"Who—who do they think . . . ?" she asks Ryan, her voice trailing off.

"Please tell me this means they found and locked up the killer for life," I say, nearly choking on the words.

Ryan shakes his head.

"It was only forensics that determined the weapon. Now the cops are on a mad search for it. I just hope it leads them to the bastard who did this, and then the nightmare can be over."

"It won't ever be over for the people who loved him, though," I say. "It'll never be over for us."

Ryan nods, reaching his arm over my shoulder.

"I know."

Brianne raises an eyebrow at me, and I wince as it dawns on me what she's thinking. *You confided in this guy about you and Chace and kept me in the dark?* I clearly have more explaining to do.

And then I sense someone else approaching. I feel the heat of her stare before I see her. I can smell the floral perfume, a scent I once loved that's now turned sour. Do I dare look up?

I meet her eyes. There she is, Lana Rivera, her face pallid against the curtain of dark hair, her red-rimmed eyes flashing with fury. Ryan drops his arm from my shoulder, and even Brianne steps back an inch.

"Lana." I reach my hand toward her—for what, I'm not sure. Maybe I want to end this; maybe I only have energy for one fight. But she flinches as if I've struck her. And then she spits on the floor in front of me.

"Hey!" The security guard springs into action, yanking her away from me. "I'm reporting you for this."

She laughs bitterly, pushing the guard's arm off her. And then she's gone.

I turn to Ryan and Brianne, shivering.

"You guys probably don't want to be seen with me."

"Maybe not," Ryan says, forcing a grim smile. "But Chace would want us to stick up for you."

The security guard returns, planting himself at my side.

"You okay, miss? Do you feel up to going to class?"

"Of course not," I say. "But I don't have a choice, do I? So let's just go."

• • •

I thought my first day back after my accident last semester was as bad as it could get. Back then, I couldn't imagine anything comparing to the gasps of classmates seeing my face for the first time, or the many conversations that cut short the second I walked past. But oh, was I wrong. At least in those days, people pretended to care about me. Today, the moment with Lana is just the tip of the iceberg. I might as well have a scarlet letter branded across my chest, or something worse. Because, as Brianne murmurs to me during Shakespearean Lit, there's a sick rumor going around that *I* killed Chace out of anger when he refused to dump Lana for me. It's ironically clear who must have started that rumor.

Brianne asks if I want to join her and the girls from orchestra at lunch, but I can tell she's just being nice. She doesn't actually want to sit with me in the eye of the storm, surrounded by all those blatant stares and pointed fingers. Who would?

"Thanks, but it's okay," I tell her. "I have so much work to catch up on. I think I'll just go to the library."

On my way there, at the top floor of Academics Hall, I run into Stephanie, Lana's best friend—someone I once called a friend myself. She's walking alongside the guy I remember as her on-again off-again fling from last year, Ben Forrester, and she pushes roughly past me, the sharp end of her binder jabbing me in the ribs.

"Hey, Ben, did you hear the cops are searching all the rooms in the school right now for the weapon?" she says loudly, clearly for my ears and not Ben's. "I'd be *real* nervous if I were a certain Nicole Morgan."

My cheeks flame. By the time I reach the library, I've lost my barely-there appetite, and I toss my sandwich. It feels wrong, anyway, to think of things like eating, drinking, studying, and sleeping—it's not right that we should be going about the mundane details of our lives, when Chace doesn't get to anymore.

Afternoon is when I leave academics behind, and the latter half of my school day is taken up by advanced music courses for the Virtuoso Program. I hold my breath as I enter the choir room, unsure if these classmates will be as vicious to me as the others. But from the moment Professor Teller greets me with a big hug, I know that here at least, I am safe. She keeps me busy during the three-hour block of classes, giving me a tricky Shostakovich solo to learn and choral singers to accompany, on top of rehearsing my planned pieces for the Orchestra Showcase, which includes an exhilarating duo number with Brianne on cello. For these three hours, in my bubble of music, I can almost forget. Almost. But the ringing of the bell at three o'clock yanks me back to reality, reminding me of what's next: my meeting with Chace's parents.

I used to often imagine what it would be like to meet them. In my daydreams, Chace held my hand proudly, introducing me as his girlfriend, and Congressman and Mrs. Porter's eyes lit up as they felt the love between us, exchanging a glance that said it all. *Thank God he found the right one.*

I never had a scar in those daydreams. My face was un-blemished, my spirit unshaken. It was certainly never part of the plan to meet the Porters by detective escort, with my mom joining me for "protection." But that is my current reality. At least I was able to talk John Sanford into letting Mom and me handle this one on our own. The thought of meeting Chace's parents with a lawyer in tow made my stom-ach coil, made me feel guilty of . . . something.

We're supposed to meet Congressman and Mrs. Porter at the Alumni Club, the exclusive space on the basement floor of Academics Hall. I've never been inside, and at any other time in my life, it would have been a thrill. The place is leg-endary; it's been described as our equivalent of the final clubs and secret societies of Ivy League lore. It's not enough to just be alumni—to get a key to the lounge, you need to have made a name for yourself out there in the world. You have to be invited. And now I'm getting a peek behind the curtain, but for the worst possible reason.

I meet Detective Kimble and Mom in the dressing room adjacent to the Joyce Hall theater, the place we determined would draw the least amount of attention. I grab my cap from my backpack and slip on my sunglasses. It's not much of a disguise, but it makes me feel less exposed.

Detective Kimble leads the two of us back out onto the quad and up the steps into Academics Hall, where she unlocks an inconspicuous door across from the janitorial closet. To my surprise, the door opens onto an antique French elevator.

Until now, I've only seen elevators like this in old photographs. It must date from the school's origins. The creaky elevator sputters us down to the basement and in front of a recessed doorway. Detective Kimble slips a card into the slot, and the door swings open. We find ourselves standing in the middle of a Victorian fantasy of a parlor, made up of mahogany mirrored walls, royal blue brocade curtains, antique furniture, and hanging candelabras. A bust of the school's founder is displayed on a marble pillar at the entrance.

Mom and I follow Detective Kimble farther into the room, where a couple is seated on a blue-and-gold damask couch, their backs to us as they hold each other. A man in a black suit stands off to the side, staring straight ahead. My stomach lurches.

This must be the congressman and his wife, along with their security detail. The moment I once looked forward to, and now dread, is here. I shut my eyes momentarily, willing myself to feel Chace's hand squeezing mine. But there's nothing there.

Detective Kimble clears her throat. Congressman and Mrs. Porter turn around, still clutching each other's hands. They are dressed in black, their expressions deadened as they look at me. They seem to have aged another ten years since I saw them at the candlelight vigil.

"Congressman, Mrs. Porter," Detective Kimble begins. "I've brought Nicole Morgan, and this is her mother, Ms. Lindsey Morgan."

Mom finds her voice before I do.

"We're so incredibly sorry for your loss," she says, stepping forward with her hand outstretched. "My daughter and I are both heartbroken. We can only imagine what you're going through."

Congressman Porter nods slightly. He shakes her hand and then mine, while Mrs. Porter simply sits beside him, staring at us with watery eyes. I can't tell what she's thinking.

"Have a seat," he instructs us.

"Can I get you any coffee, Congressman?" Detective Kimble offers, her voice far sweeter than it's ever been with me.

"We'll take two, please, with no cream. Thank you." He glances at us. "Would you like anything?"

"No, thanks," I murmur. I know there's no way I'll manage to keep anything down in my current state.

"I'll take the same, thank you," Mom says. Detective Kimble smiles tightly, not quite as eager to please when it comes to the two of us.

After she disappears down the hall to the club's kitchen, the four of us sit in a momentary silence, eyeing each other. Finally, I manage to speak.

"I always hoped to meet you, but in such a different way. You saw the pictures, so you know what . . . what Chace and I meant to each other."

"That's what we're struggling to understand," Congressman Porter says, rubbing his forehead with his palm. "Our son was dating Lana Rivera, for almost a year. He never mentioned you."

The words are a slap across my face. I drop my gaze, cheeks burning. That can't be right.

"But he said he did—he said he told you about us last spring, when he was planning to break it off with her." I remember it so clearly, the mixture of relief and terror I felt upon learning that they knew about us. Is it possible Chace was only appeasing me and didn't tell them the truth after all? Or are the Porters the ones lying?

"No, he didn't say a thing. And he didn't break it off with Lana, either, did he?" the congressman counters.

"There were reasons for that," I say stiffly. "On both sides."

I catch Mrs. Porter's eyes fixating on my scar, and I have the nagging sense that Chace did tell them the truth, that they're only pretending to be in the dark. But *why?*

My mom speaks up. "Sir, there's no reason to question my daughter's honesty." I can practically hear her gritting her teeth. "The photos speak for themselves. Our kids cared a great deal about each other."

Detective Kimble reappears, holding a tray laden with three steaming mugs of coffee. After she sets them down in front of the Porters and my mom, the congressman leans forward, his head bowed.

"I'm asking because there's a theory out there. I'm hoping it's not true. It's that you and my son never had any relation-

ship, that you Photoshopped those pictures. And when he refused you—"

"Stop!" I leap to my feet, incredulous at what I'm hearing. "Whatever you heard, it's all lies. If you need more proof,
there's plenty of it. Chace kept all the letters we wrote to
each other, they're in his dorm." I turn to Detective Kimble.
"And aren't you checking phone records or something? It's all
there!"

Detective Kimble eyes me carefully.

"The search of his room hasn't turned up anything about
you yet. And there's no correspondence between the two of
you from this week."

"This *week*? It was last spring that we were together."

Mom stands up, wrapping a protective arm around my
shoulder.

"I'm sure the two of you are hurting in ways I can't possibly understand," she says quietly. "But that doesn't give you
any right to accuse my daughter."

"Talk to Chace's roommate, Ryan," I burst out, the idea
coming to me like a beacon of hope. "He knows everything.
He'll tell you it's all true, that whatever he had with Lana,
Chace loved me." A tear rolls down my cheek, and I roughly
wipe it away. "And I love him."

Mrs. Porter, who still hasn't spoken a word, reaches
across the space between us and touches my hand. *Is she trying to comfort me?*

"Can we trust you?" she asks softly.

There's something about her voice. I can't seem to place it, but it reminds me of something—a certain feeling of dread.

Or maybe I'm going crazy.

"Of course you can trust me," I answer. "I'm telling you the truth."

"Do you need anything else?" Mom asks curtly.

Congressman Porter opens his mouth to say more, but then glances at his wife and shakes his head. "That's enough for now."

"Good. Once again, we're sorry for your loss."

"I'll show you out," Detective Kimble says, her eyes flicking between me and the Porters.

Mom and I follow her to the door. Just before we reach it, I turn around.

"Chace would want me to play at the funeral." My voice wobbles, but I don't back down, looking straight into his parents' eyes. "He loved my music, maybe more than anyone else. I have to give him one last song."

Without waiting for an answer, I turn and follow my mom and the detective through the door.

I can't bear to hear a no.

• • •

Mom drops me off at my dorm, hugging me good night before departing for her hotel a few miles from campus.

"Are you sure you wouldn't rather I sleep here tonight?" she asks for the third time.

I force a smile.

"That's sweet of you, but there's barely any room for both of us. I'll just see you tomorrow. I love you."

She kisses my forehead.

"I love you, too, honey. We'll get through this together. I promise."

After she closes the door behind her, I throw open my desk drawer. If Detective Kimble didn't find the letters in Chace's room, is there any chance he could have returned them to me, without my knowing—?

A scream rings in my ears, ice flooding my veins.

I'm shivering, shaking. I can't be seeing this.

It can't be real.

I hear the footsteps of the security guard from down the hall, and I lunge toward the door, heart in my throat as I turn the lock.

"Everything all right in there, miss?" The guard raps on the door twice. It dawns on me that I must have screamed out loud.

"F-fine!" I call out, my voice shrill with panic. "I just—it was just a spider, but I, um, took care of it."

I wait until his footsteps retreat, and then I dive back to the desk. *Please let it be gone now. Please let it have been just a hallucination,* I pray silently.

But there it is, unmistakable in the middle of my desk drawer: a thick kitchen knife, covered with crusted blood.

The thought of that blade plunging into the skin and soul

I loved makes me want to rip this entire room to shreds. My arms and legs begin to tingle, my vision turning hazy, and I know from past experience that this is the start of a panic attack. But I can't afford to give in to it now. I need to think straight.

Someone clearly planted the weapon in my room. But they were a day late. If they'd done it yesterday, when Detective Kimble searched my things, I would have been arrested on the spot. I shudder in horror.

My mind races as I stare at the weapon. If I turn it in and explain that I'm being set up, maybe the cops will be able to use DNA on the knife to find out who did this to Chace.

Or . . . No one will believe that I was being set up. I could be arrested the second I make the call to Detective Kimble.

I grab my phone to dial Mom, but hang up as soon as it occurs to me that this is not a conversation I can afford anyone lingering outside my door to hear.

"Chace," I whisper into the air, my throat thick with tears. "I need you so much right now. I don't know what to do."

But of course, there's no answer. *Why do I keep thinking Chace's spirit will help me?* I can't get lost in these hopeful delusions; I need to figure out a plan. Now. I pace my room, hands trembling as I eye the sickening weapon in my desk. What am I going to do, what am I going to *do*?

Whoever planted it in my room clearly intends for me to be caught with it—and if they grow impatient waiting, all they need to do is call in a tip to Detective Kimble. I have to get it out of my room, that's the only way to save myself from being framed. But then . . . isn't moving the evidence a crime in and of itself?

I slump onto the bed, head in my hands. There's no good solution, only one choice. I have to get the knife out of my room—but I'll leave it someplace where the cops can find it and trace it back to the real killer. I hope.

The thought of touching the evil object turns my stomach. I need music—I need to pretend this is a performance, that it isn't real.

I plug my earbuds into my phone and cue up a playlist. Dario Marianelli's *Atonement* score couldn't be more fitting. I exhale as the piano begins with a staccato pulse, like notes of warning, and then the frenetic strings color in the melody. I close my eyes. Yes, I'm just playing a part. This isn't real.

I grab my winter gloves from my dresser drawer and slip them onto my hands. Just as I'm reaching for the knife, looking away so I don't have to see myself touch it, the music in my earbuds comes to a halt—replaced with the sound of a muffled yet familiar voice.

"Find me at our spot."

My heart leaps, daring my mind to believe.

"Chace? Is that you?"

The pulsating piano and strings of *Atonement* resume playing, but all I hear is the echo of his last words. *". . . our spot . . ."* I want so much to trust this, but can I? Or have I entered full-blown hallucination territory? I'm all out of options.

I glance from the door to the window, but it's not like I have a choice. The window is my only way out unseen. Thankfully, I'm only on the fourth floor.

Holding my breath, I take the knife into my gloved hands. Even through the fabric, I can feel the cruel blade burning against my palm. I drop it as fast as I can into a ziplock bag and stuff it into my backpack. Then, lifting my backpack onto my shoulders, I unlatch the window.

Cold air rushes to greet me. With a silent prayer, I squeeze my body through the opening and crawl out to the other side of the windowsill, latching onto the narrow railing that lines the building's exterior. It's a balancing act, and as I climb down, it occurs to me at the worst possible moment that if someone else's window is open on this side of the building—it'll all be over. I quicken my pace, pushing my body down the railing until I pass the third floor, then the second and the first, finally landing on my knees in the grass. As far as I can tell, no one saw me. Thank God.

I forgot to bring a flashlight in my haste, so I move through the grounds in the dark, letting the stars guide my way, and ducking behind a tree anytime I think I hear a security guard's footsteps. Luckily, it seems Headmaster Higgins has them stationed primarily outside the campus gates and within the buildings—so the grounds are free.

The gurgle of water beneath the wooden bridge lets me know that I'm close. My pulse quickens, my mind racing, as I wonder what I'm about to find. Will it be Chace's spirit, responding to my plea for help? Will it be another vision like the other night? Or . . . could it be something else entirely?

"Nicole."

And with a gasp, I turn around.

PART TWO
NICOLE + CHACE

hear they're going to arrest her soon. That's what my mom says, anyway. She says the cops on the case are getting all their ducks in a row, but Nicole is the lead suspect. "No one's even thinking about you, mija," Mom said last night, running her cool palm across my forehead.

If I did do it, no one would know. Not with Nicole as the distraction. It's gratifying to go on TMZ and the other gossip sites and see what people really think of her. When the pictures leaked, I have to admit, my first instinct was fear. What if people saw the photos and assumed it was true love between the two of them (ew) and that *I* was the bad guy keeping the star-crossed lovers apart? But it's amazing what a well-placed rumor can do. I never should have worried, not with Congresswoman Diana Rivera as my mother. She's already whipped the votes. Everyone's on my side. They all believe Nicole faked the pictures or blackmailed him, or something else equally twisted. They even have nicknames for her in the press: "The Girl in the Picture" and "The Phantom of the Philharmonic." That last one's my favorite.

I actually ran into her yesterday in the halls. She was walking with that boring orchestra friend of hers and Ryan Wyatt, of all people—I *knew* I never liked him—and when our eyes met, I swear I thought I might kill her. I wanted to take my manicured fingernails and claw them into that scar of hers. To think I used to consider her a *friend*—that I let a nerd like her into my world, into my parties and my family and my childhood home. And then she went and betrayed me.

No one ever betrayed me until those two.

The truth is, hating Nicole is just what I need right now. It keeps my mind trained on anger, instead of sadness and grief. Because if I really let myself stop and think about what happened to Chace, that he's gone forever . . . well, I just might not recover from that. And a Rivera always recovers.

My alarm clock buzzes, and I slam it off with my fist. I've been up for hours, anyway. Today is Chace's funeral, and I'm giving a speech. An unpleasant memory pushes forward, clamoring for my attention. The congressman called last night, telling me Nicole asked if she could play the violin at the service. She actually had the nerve.

"I wonder if we should let her," Congressman Porter said over the phone, his voice sounding ragged. "She was quite insistent that it's what Chace would have wanted."

Yes, I know he was obsessed with the girl's talent. But there was no way I was about to let Nicole take over Chace's funeral.

"She's just pushing in," I told the congressman. "I think it would be wrong to include her."

So it'll be just five of us taking the podium today: Chace's dad, his little brother, Teddy, me, Headmaster Higgins, and Ryan, who somehow snuck onto the program. Mrs. Porter is too distraught to speak, so the congressman will be giving the eulogy on behalf of both of them.

I hear stirring from the bed on the other side of the room. Stephanie rolls over, rubbing her eyes.

"You awake, Lan?"

"Obviously."

She props herself up on her elbow.

"I know how hard this day is going to be. I'm so sorry."

I nod.

"I should start getting ready."

Mom bought me a new black dress for today, thinking Chanel might cheer me up. I wonder what Chace would think if he saw me in it.

I wonder if he still thought I was as beautiful at the end as he did in the beginning.

• • •

My dad took the train from DC to join Mom and me at the funeral, and the sight of his stalwart figure beside us, those warm brown eyes looking down on me with concern, gives me a sense of relief. Mom is the one who gets things done, who protects me like the mama bear she is, but you don't go crying on her shoulder. My dad is the one who allows me to let my guard down. He's the parent who sees my fractured heart and tries to put it back together. If only he could.

We get to the church early, giving us a few moments alone with the Porters before the public enters. The sight of Teddy's tearstained cheeks and Mrs. Porter's hollow expression is a stark reminder of everything I've been burying down deep. He's gone. And there's no going back in time to make things right.

My eyes fly to the altar, stomach clenching as I brace myself for a casket, until I remember. There's no body anymore. Only ashes. A large canvas photo of Chace stands at the altar in place of a casket, surrounded by white carnations. I drop my gaze to the ground, blinking back the fire behind my eyes.

The Porters greet my parents with dazed handshakes, while I hug all three of them tightly, flashing back to the first time I met Chace's parents. It hurts to remember how happy I was that night at the restaurant, flush in the glow of new romance. I never could have imagined how it would all unravel. If I had, I'd have marched straight into Headmaster Higgins's office and demanded a different roommate, *any* roommate but her. Because one thing's for sure: if it weren't for our friendship, Nicole would never have gotten within spitting distance of a guy like Chace.

My parents and I lower into the seats in our reserved pew behind the Porters, watching the rest of the mourners file in. Stephanie and Kara arrive soon after us, and they sit right behind me, Steph squeezing my shoulder in solidarity. The guys from Chace's soccer team are part of the next batch of arrivals, taking up a whole pew on the other side of the aisle. I feel someone slide into the seat beside me, and I stiffen. It's Ryan, of course. One of Nicole's last defenders. Why does he have to sit here?

As if he can read my mind, he says, "The reverend asked me to sit up front, since I'm one of the speakers. . . . How are you doing?"

"How do you think?" I ask, my tone coming out even frostier than I intended.

He winces.

"I know. I feel the same." He glances at my mom and dad, who are deep in conversation with someone from Congress who's just joined our pew. "You're lucky you have your parents here."

"Yeah. Are yours coming?"

Ryan lowers his eyes.

"They couldn't get off work. Plus there was no one to watch my brother."

Our conversation, if you can call it that, ends there. The church is soon filled to standing room only, and the heavy doors swing shut. I turn around in my seat and scan the crowd, breathing a sigh of relief when I find no trace of Nicole, not even sitting with Brianne and the other orchestra geeks in the back pew. I warned the Porters that she would be a distraction. Thankfully, they must have listened to me.

The service begins with the reverend asking us to open our prayer books, and he speaks of how all death has a purpose. *What purpose is there in this?* I want to scream, but of course I don't. I sit like the polite, well-bred girl I'm expected to be, prayer book open in my lap.

Headmaster Higgins takes the podium next, and after extolling Chace's virtues on and off the school soccer field, she reads a letter of condolence from the president of the United States. I wonder what Chace would make of that. He loved to poke fun at our parents' high and mighty jobs, but I wonder if he'd be proud now, hearing the president acknowledging his too-short life.

The headmaster returns to her seat, and all too soon it's my turn. My legs feel oddly jellylike as I stand up. Dad gives my hand a squeeze before I make my way out of our pew and walk up the aisle to the podium.

"I used to imagine being in a church like this one day with Chace," I begin. "Maybe it was silly to think that of a high-school love. But that's how I felt."

And it's true, that's exactly what I envisioned, until she came and shattered the fantasy. My throat tightens, but I continue.

"Many of you knew Chace as the star athlete of our

school, or as the congressman's handsome son, but to me he was something else entirely. He was the guy who gave me constant butterflies, who made me feel like each day was a gift." I close my eyes. "Until one day it wasn't."

For a moment it feels like I'm watching a scene in a movie, that these words are coming from an actress's mouth—because it can't be real, he can't be dead. I blink, finding my parents' faces in the crowd, and they nod their encouragement.

"I'll miss Chace Porter every day, but I'd like to believe a part of him will stay with me, in my heart, forever."

I climb down the stairs, swallowing the lump in my throat. What would he think of my eulogy from up there in heaven? Would he laugh at my so-called desire for him to stay with me, in my heart? *"Even a spirit can't split itself in two, Lana,"* he might say. *"You know whom I'd choose to be with, even in death."* My hands tighten into fists at the thought.

As I slip back into my seat, Ryan gets up, taking my place at the podium. He has a typewritten sheet of paper in his grasp.

"One of the luckiest things to ever happen to me was getting Chace Porter for a roommate," he says, looking out at the crowd. "He made the past year one that was full of adventure, fun, and friendship, and I'll never forget him. . . ."

My mind drifts as Ryan speaks. I don't care what he has to say, anyway. Instead, I replay my memories of Chace on a loop, while staring at the giant photo of his beautiful face. And then a change in Ryan's tone gets my attention.

"There was a song Chace loved. I'll never hear it again without thinking of him. You'll know it as 'Lovesong' by the Cure. If you listen carefully, you just might hear it."

And then, from outside the closed church doors, I hear the faint strains of a violin. The congregation turns around in their seats, the Porters standing up at the sound. I wait, rage rising up inside me, willing the reverend or someone else to run outside and tell Nicole to shut up, to tell her she's ruining the service. But no one does. Everyone listens in rapt silence, just like that night at our New Year's party. Congressman Porter holds his clasped hands up to his chest, while Mrs. Porter hugs Teddy close, the two of them gulping back tears. Looking around, I can't see a dry eye in the room. And then, as her violin hits a swooping, piercing note, I feel something crack inside me. I give in to my own tears, head in my hands.

Even as I hate her, she can still make me cry.

13

NICOLE

Dear Chace,

It was the train that brought us together, wasn't it? Before we found ourselves on the same Long Island Rail Road heading west, all you were to me was Lana's sweet boyfriend and I'm sure I was nothing more to you than her violin-playing roommate. But the train exposed everything, diving beneath the layers of those roles to who we really are. Do you regret it now, taking the same train as me? Sometimes I do. Only because I never meant to hurt anyone. And because now I know what it means to truly hurt, myself.

I love you still,

Nicole

JUNIOR YEAR

Midway into my train ride from Long Island to Manhattan, I spot a familiar flash of golden-brown hair, just visible above the top of the seat three rows ahead of me. It doesn't occur to me that Chace could be trying to avoid any notice, or that he might want privacy. He's a friendly face, so of course I get up from my seat, lugging my violin case behind me to join his row.

"Hi, Chace."

His head jerks up at my approach. His cheeks fill with color, but he doesn't look nearly as surprised to see me as I am to see him.

"Lana didn't mention you were going into the city, too." I slide in beside him. "We could have shared a cab to the train station."

"She doesn't know," he says quietly. "She thinks I'm at practice."

He doesn't say it, but I can tell by the look in his eyes what he's asking. He doesn't want me to tell.

"Why?" I ask. "Are you planning a surprise for her or something?" That seems like the kind of thing guys would do for a girl like Lana.

"Yeah." He nods.

"Say no more." I smile at him. "My lips are sealed."

"What about you?" He glances down at my violin case. "Doing something music-related?"

"It's my first day of rehearsals for the Philharmonic showcase," I tell him, unable to keep from beaming. He grins back.

"Oh, right. That's crazy awesome. What are you playing? Any chance it's the song from New Year's Eve?"

"'Summertime'? That's the song I auditioned with, so maybe. I guess I'll find out today." I stretch my arms over my head, giddy with a combination of excitement and nerves. He watches me and chuckles.

"It's cool how you don't hide it."

"Don't hide what?" I ask.

"How much this means to you," Chace says, turning in his seat to face me. "I'm used to people downplaying everything."

A piece of advice Lana recently gave me flashes in my mind. *You shouldn't be so obvious, Nicole.*

"Yeah, I'm not the queen of subtle," I agree.

"Don't change." He touches my arm for the briefest second before turning back to the window. And I could swear he has the same look on his face that he had the night of the meteor shower—the expression that made me feel like he saw too much when he looked at me, that made me want to push him in Lana's direction instead.

We sit in a companionable silence for the rest of the ride, my earbuds in as I mentally prepare for my first rehearsal. When it's time to change trains at Jamaica Station, we step off the platform together and find two seats next to each other in the second car. But when the train stops at Atlantic Terminal, I'm surprised to see Chace get up.

"That's my stop."

"I thought you were going into the city. Wouldn't that be Penn Station, like me?"

"I'm actually going to Brooklyn." He pauses. "Maybe we can take the train back together, though. Which one are you taking?"

"Probably the six o'clock," I reply. "Rehearsal is four hours."

"Cool. I'll already be on the train when you get here," he tells me. "I'll see you then."

"See you."

I watch as he jumps over the gap onto the platform, disappearing into a mass of commuters. And for some reason I don't yet understand, the thought of meeting him again on the train makes my pulse quicken with anticipation.

• • •

A smile spreads across my face as I skip out of the subway station and emerge in front of Lincoln Center. I can't help laughing with joy as I race up the steps to the grand plaza, taking in the buildings I've long dreamed about seeing in person. The Metropolitan Opera House faces me straight ahead, its marquee announcing a performance of *La Bohème* starring Renée Fleming herself, while Koch Theater, home of *the* New York City Ballet, stands to its left. Opposite is my wished-for home,

Dand Geffen Hall, theater of the New York Philharmonic. Tears spring to my eyes, and I race toward it.

"Whoa!" A cute boy about my age, with dark skin and short black hair, holds up his arms before I nearly plow into his cello. "Watch it!"

"Sorry, sorry!" My cheeks flush with embarrassment. *Great first impression, Nicole!*

"It's okay," he says with a grin. "You're clearly in more of a rush to get to rehearsal than I am. I'm Damien Bell, by the way."

So *this* is the player who took the cellist spot Brianne auditioned for. Maybe I should give him the cold shoulder out of respect for my friend—but I'm too jubilant to pull it off.

"Hi." I reach out my hand to shake his. "I'm Nicole Morgan. Tell me, should I be more nervous?"

He laughs.

"Only if you mind teachers who work you to death."

"Well, *that* I'm used to," I tell him. "Have you heard of Oyster Bay Prep?"

"Oh yeah." He opens the door for me and we walk through. "I've heard it's almost as rough there as where I go, LaGuardia."

I stop as we enter the building, my mouth falling open at the gilded lobby.

"*This* is where we're going to rehearse?" I marvel.

"Wait'll you see the theater. You're never going to want to leave." He gives me a deadpan look. "Just remember, not everyone gets asked back the following year. So if you want to keep your place in the showcase, you'd better own it and be at *least* as good as me."

For a minute I think he's actually that pompous, but then he bursts out laughing.

"I kid, I kid! Don't worry, the vibe here is surprisingly much more *Friends* than *Black Swan*."

"Good to know," I say with a giggle.

We walk into the theater still chuckling—and I know I'm going to love it here.

• • •

Chace is waiting for me in the same row we sat in earlier when I board the Long Island Rail Road, just like he said he would be. Still, I can't help feeling a flicker of surprise at the sight of him. I guess there's something surreal about seeing him apart from Lana, when the two of them have coexisted in my mind since the day I met them in the auditorium.

"Looks like rehearsal went well," he says as I slide in beside him.

"How can you tell?" I ask, touching my flushed cheeks.

He studies me, a teasing glint in his eye.

"I sense a definite spring in your step."

"It was incredible. To be with the best young players in the country, rehearsing in one of the most legendary theaters in the world, with Franz Lindgren himself conducting us . . ." I pinch my arm. "Yup. Not a dream! And I made a friend, this really great guy, Damien. It's just awesome to meet people passionate about the same things as me, you know?"

Chace's expression changes, but he keeps smiling.

"That's awesome, Nicole."

"Anyway, sorry to gush so much. But you probably know what I mean, what with your soccer."

"Don't apologize. I do know what you mean," he says. "There's something really special about knowing what you're supposed to do, and finding your tribe."

"Exactly," I agree.

Chace pats my arm gently.

"I'm glad everything is working out for you, Nicole. You deserve it."

"Thanks. That's nice of you."

His eyes remain on mine. I feel an unexpected jolt in my chest, my cheeks growing inexplicably warm. I quickly change the subject.

"How did it go for you today?" I wiggle my eyebrows. "You know, Lana's surprise?"

He smiles and looks away.

"All went smoothly. I'll tell you more . . . when I can."

remember exactly when my boyfriend started acting differently. What burns the most is how, out of all my friends, Nicole is the one I chose to confide in about it. I remember how she brushed off my concerns, told me she was sure it was nothing, that everything was as great as ever between us. And all along, it was her.

I'm lying in my dorm room in the dark, even though it's the middle of the day and I'm technically supposed to be in Political Science right now. But I can't bring myself to sit through another pointless class. This whole school week has been all screwed up, anyway, with some classes canceled altogether and others half empty. How are you supposed to deal with the sudden death—*murder*—of a student? Is there any right way?

My phone buzzes with a text, and I roll over to retrieve it. The message is from Mom, who, amazingly, still hasn't returned to DC yet. She must be *really* worried about me.

I'm coming to your room. Are you alone?

Yes, I type back.

No less than ten minutes later, she's bursting into my dorm, her couture pantsuit looking ridiculously out of place in these surroundings.

"They found the weapon," she says as soon as she enters, her brow covered in sweat.

I freeze.

"What? Where?"

"Under the bleachers of the soccer field," Mom says. "It's all over the news."

"But . . ." I swallow hard. "Why wouldn't the cops have found it the first time they looked, if it was there all along?"

"I don't know, mija. But they're going to be fingerprinting everyone in the school, even the teachers, to see if they can find a match on the knife. That's why I'm here." She takes a deep breath. "Are you going to be okay getting your prints taken?"

I stare at her, the realization dawning on me.

"Why wouldn't I be? What are you afraid of?" She doesn't answer, and I press on. "Do you think I *did it,* Mom? Do you actually think that?"

"Shh!" Mom clamps her hand over my mouth, her eyes flashing with panic. "You can't say things like that out loud. What if someone overhears and gets the wrong idea?"

"Okay, sorry!"

She lets go of me and starts pacing my dorm room.

"I imagine they'll start taking fingerprints as soon as possible. I wanted to prepare you."

"Thanks," I say dully.

"Your father is taking the train back to DC late tonight," she says, switching the topic abruptly. "Why don't you join us for dinner at the hotel before he leaves? It'll probably be good for you to get out of this environment."

"Fine. Hey, Mom?"

She pauses.

"Yes?"

"Do you still think they're going to arrest Nicole?"

She gives me a contemplative look.

"Yes, mija. I'd be surprised if they have their eye on anyone else, and if the fingerprints match, well . . . then her goose is cooked."

The words are so confident, yet the look in her eyes betrays her fear. I wonder, as I lean my head back and try to remember that night, if I should be afraid, too.

• • •

As it turns out, I'm not free to go to dinner with my parents, or to set foot anywhere outside of campus tonight. A couple hours after my mom comes bearing her warning, there's a rough knock on my door. I open it and find one of the school's new security guards, handing me a typewritten sheet of paper.

"Everyone's required in the dining hall tonight," he tells me, before moving on to the next door.

Stephanie, who's back from class and busily texting Ben Forrester, glances up from her phone.

"What's going on?"

Instead of replying, I just hand her the paper. She sits up straighter, reading it aloud.

"Due to new key evidence found in the Chace Porter case, we require every student and teacher to be present at dinner tonight. You will be taken in groups of twenty to have your fingerprints scanned, after which time you will be free to return to your meals. We've enlisted security guards to retrieve and escort any student or teacher who fails to show up, so please do us the courtesy of arriving on time.

Thank you, Headmaster Higgins"

Steph stares at me, her eyes wide.

"This sounds serious. If what everyone's saying is true, then this is going to be the final nail in Nicole's coffin, huh?"

I bite my fingernail, a childhood habit that's resurfaced this week.

"Let's hope so."

• • •

Stepping into the dining hall that night, Stephanie and I are met by a sea of panicky faces. Apparently, the headmaster's letter scared most of our classmates into not just showing up, but showing up early.

The whole space is reconfigured, with the two long dining tables in the back serving as fingerprinting stations manned by uniformed cops, while the rest of the dining hall retains its usual purpose. But of course, the trays of food go untouched.

"What were they thinking, combining this with *dinner*?" Stephanie mutters in my ear.

A young woman swoops down on us, dressed in plain-clothes and a badge around her neck that reads OFFICER SIMONE.

"Hello, girls. Please sign in here." She holds out a clip-board, and Stephanie scribbles our names. "You'll be in group six, straight ahead. When I call your number, your group will get fingerprinted, and then you can go back to your table for dinner."

Yeah, right. Fat chance of me eating at a time like this.

I follow the direction Officer Simone is pointing in, and a block of ice sets in my stomach. *She* is there, her scarred face even paler than usual. Nicole is sitting between Brianne and a woman I recognize as her mom from the framed picture she used to keep on her side of the nightstand.

Catching my expression, Stephanie gives the officer a pleading look.

"Isn't there another group—?"

"This isn't social time, ladies," she snaps. "Go on now."

I watch Officer Simone saunter off, feeling my face heat up with rage. The woman clearly doesn't know who I am.

"There's Kara." Stephanie links her arm with mine, gently steering us to the opposite end of the table from Nicole. I can feel all eyes on us, our classmates watching with bated breath as Nicole and I are forced to share the same table. Kara slides down the bench to make room as we approach.

"How are you holding up, Lan?" She gives me a tight hug. "God, can you believe this?"

I shake my head. "No."

We watch in silence as the two cops manning the finger-printing tables go down the line of students, each of our classmates placing their index finger on a silicon surface. A smattering of teachers are mixed in among them, and it's weird to see how frightened everyone looks, young and old alike. It's as though every one of us harbors a secret fear that we could be found guilty.

"Group six!" Officer Simone barks into a microphone.

I hang back with Stephanie and Kara as everyone in our group makes their reluctant way to the fingerprinting table. This is one occasion where I definitely don't want to be first in line.

As we move up, I find myself studying Nicole, who's toward the front, clutching Brianne's hand. She looks like she hasn't eaten in days, her figure weak enough to snap. Is the weight loss from grief or guilt? Or both?

It's her turn. I watch her attempt to take a breath, and

then place her finger on the scanner. And as I watch, a memory flashes in my mind.

I slap my note onto the tree, jabbing it in place with a thumbtack. I stand back, surveying my handiwork.

DID YOU REALLY THINK I'D EVER FORGIVE YOU? WHAT A JOKE! HOPE YOU'RE NOT STILL SCARED OF THE WOODS, BECAUSE NO ONE IS COMING FOR YOU. YOU'RE ALL ALONE, JUST LIKE YOU DESERVE TO BE.

I kick my shoe into the dirt, sending up a spray of soil as the anger floods me anew. I turn on my heel, breaking into a run as I leave the woods behind.

I blink rapidly, trying to shut out the image in my mind, but another is quick to follow.

She walks through the classroom door, and I can barely breathe at the sight. It's worse than I imagined. A long, jagged mark runs down the length of her cheek, surrounded by puffy, purple-bruised skin. For a moment she meets my eyes, and panic bubbles in my chest. If anyone were to ever find out the truth about that night . . . I can't even think about it, I'd be in such deep shit. But she looks away, and then I know. My secret is safe.

Besides, she has to realize—it's all her own fault.

A wave of nausea washes over me as the memory passes, along with another feeling I didn't expect.

"I need to get out of here," I blurt out to Kara and Stephanie.

"We're up next," Kara tells me. "It'll be over in a second."

"Lana, you're all sweaty." Stephanie hands me a tissue,

just as Kara gives me a gentle nudge forward. And suddenly I'm face-to-face with a police officer.

"All right, miss, place your finger directly on the scanner," the officer says in the bored tone of someone doing this all day.

"Okay."

My finger hits the scanner as I hold my breath.

Our rehearsals for the Philharmonic Contemporary Youth Showcase take place every Saturday and Sunday for the next three weeks, so today I find myself once again boarding the Long Island Rail Road into Manhattan. The last thing I expect is to see Chace Porter joining me on the train platform, as if commuting together is our new normal. But there he is.

"Hey," he greets me, in the casual tone of someone who doesn't seem to find this coincidence as surprising as I do.

"Hi. Brooklyn again?" I ask.

He nods.

"Must be some surprise you're planning." I smile as my stomach gives a slight twinge. It must be amazing to be cared for the way he cares about Lana.

Just then, the train hurtles into view. Once it slows to a stop, we step off the platform and inside a car, finding a pair of seats together on the upper level.

"I was actually hoping I'd find you here," Chace says, pulling his iPhone and earbuds out of his backpack. "I remembered this old song from when I was little. My grandfather was really into music, and he used to play it all the time. He kind of raised me, with my parents being so busy. Anyway, I thought of you. I don't know, maybe it's something you might want to play."

He hands me his earbuds, and our fingers touch. I quickly move my hand as a blush creeps up my cheeks.

"That's so nice of you to think of me," I tell him. And it's true; I can't remember anyone else besides my mom or music teachers ever picking out a song for me.

Sticking the earbuds into my ears, I'm greeted by a distinctly smoky voice.

> *"Though some may reach for the stars,*
> *Others will end behind bars.*
> *What the future has in store,*
> *No one ever knows before."*

"It's Nina Simone!" I exclaim. "I love her."

He grins, and I close my eyes to listen. The rest of the world soon melts away as I fall into the song.

> *"Tomorrow is my turn,*
> *No more doubts, no more fears*

Tomorrow is my turn
When my luck is returning
All these years I've been learning
To save fingers from burning . . ."

The heartrending melody, Nina's hypnotic voice, and the gorgeous string and horn arrangements all leave me transfixed. But most of all, it's the lyrics that cut through to my soul. As the song fades out, I find I can't speak.

"The chorus just seemed written for you," Chace says, gently removing the earbuds from my ears. "*Make life worth living, now it's my life I'm living.*' I don't know—it just made me think of you, stepping into the spotlight with the Philharmonic after all these years of working so hard behind the scenes."

I shake my head in wonder.

"How is it possible that you know me so well?"

He pauses.

"I guess I just . . . see you," he says in a low voice. "I see you even when you're not there."

He didn't really just say that. Did he? I stare into his beautiful blue-gray eyes. *What is happening?*

"You do know I liked you first. Don't you?"

My heart jumps.

"What?"

"After we met that day in the theater, I kept trying to talk to you," he confesses. "But then you pushed me toward Lana, and I knew."

"Knew what?" I ask, my palms growing sweaty.

"That you weren't into me." He smiles sadly.

"I . . ." I swallow hard. "I didn't believe it. That someone like you would . . ."

The train comes to a grinding halt, cutting off my words. We're at the Atlantic Terminal station in Brooklyn. I exhale.

Chace rises to his feet. He brushes his hand against my shoulder for a brief moment before stepping off the train.

"I'm sorry. I didn't mean to freak you out."

"You didn't," I whisper. But it's a lie. My mind is swimming with images of an alternate reality, where I'm in the arms of the boy who seems to know my soul better than anyone else. And it all would have happened, if I'd only had the confidence to recognize his attention for what it was.

"Chace," I call out, just as he reaches the train door. "You're not in Brooklyn to plan a surprise for Lana, are you?"

He shakes his head, opening his mouth to say more. But the train doors close and leave us staring at each other through the window.

• • •

My mind is somewhere else entirely during rehearsal, but for some reason my playing only improves. Every time my bow descends on the strings, I see his face and the notes seem to cry out, punctuated by an emotion I've never felt before. Especially when it's time to rehearse "Summertime," the piece that got me into the showcase. I flash back to the

New Year's Eve party as I play, remembering the look on his face and our hushed conversation after. I think of Lana and my playing only grows more urgent, the strings wailing my guilt.

But there's nothing to feel guilty about, I remind myself. *I'm not going to do anything about this . . . connection with Chace. I would never hurt Lana.*

As rehearsal wraps, our conductor and teacher, Franz Lindgren, calls me downstage.

"You played with great passion today," he tells me in his thick Scandinavian accent. "Please recapture that emotion in every rehearsal."

"Thank you so much, Maestro," I say, my face flushing from his praise. Although the idea of reliving today's emotions in every rehearsal fills me with a bit of dread.

"Impressive," Damien calls out from upstage, after the conductor steps out of the theater. "Two showcases under my belt, and I still haven't gotten a shout-out from Franz Lindgren himself."

"Really?" I glance at Damien, who shoots me a grin as he packs up his cello. "Thanks. Though I definitely think you deserve some praise, too."

"You're not going to hear an argument from me there," Damien says with a chuckle, slinging his cello case over his shoulder. "See you next weekend, Nicole. Keep doing what you're doing."

• • •

There's a different energy in the air as I step onto the eastbound train, making my way to Chace's row. I hesitate before taking a seat, wondering if this is wrong, if I'm playing with fire. Is it a betrayal to Lana to keep up a friendship with Chace, now that I know how he once felt about me? But as I look in his eyes, I know I can't run away. I'm not sure I'd want to, even if I could. Still, I keep a wide berth between us.

"How was rehearsal?" he greets me, though I can tell his mind is elsewhere—just like mine.

"It was good, thanks." I look closer at him. "Are you going to tell me what you're really doing in Brooklyn?"

He pauses.

"I want to. Sometimes I think I'll go insane if I have to keep it hidden any longer."

I sit up straighter. This sounds serious.

"What is it, Chace?"

He glances out the window, avoiding my eyes.

"Do you think—would you still consider someone a good person, even if they once did something bad, something they regret every day?"

My pulse begins to race.

"It depends on what it is. But if we're talking about you here, I can't imagine anything changing my mind about you being good."

He rubs his forearms, as if the air has suddenly turned cold.

"Maybe next time . . ." He takes a deep breath. "Maybe

next time you can come with me. That's probably the—the easiest way to explain."

"Chace, isn't this something you should be doing with Lana?" I ask tentatively.

He shakes his head slightly.

"I can't."

"But she's your girlfriend," I insist, stating the obvious. "It's not right to keep secrets from her. *I* shouldn't be keeping secrets from her."

"I know," he says quietly. "I shouldn't ask that of you." But he doesn't say anything more, and we sit in silence for a few minutes.

"Okay, can I ask you something else?" I shift in my seat so my body is facing his. "It's about . . . what you told me this morning."

He nods, his expression turning shy. And for a second I'm speechless at the thought that I can make the most gorgeous guy I've ever seen shy. *Me.*

"If you—if you felt the way you said, then why were you so quick to take my suggestion and ask Lana out?" My face reddens with embarrassment as I ask the question, but I have to know.

"I'm only human. And maybe I was a little ego-bruised," he admits. "But I felt that you weren't interested, and there she was. Lana is a beautiful, great girl. I knew I'd be lucky to go out with her." He clears his throat. "I *am* lucky. It's just . . . you're different."

His words hang in the air, reverberating in my ears. *"You're different."* Normally when people say that to me, I can hear the clear subtext: *You're weird, you're a nerd, what girl your age sits in a room playing the violin all day? You should dress better, you should go outside and get a tan, you should wear makeup.* But when Chace calls me different, I know in my gut that he means it as the highest compliment. And for the first time ever, I smile at the word.

"Thank you. I'll never forget today," I tell him. "The song, and—and everything else."

"Why does this sound like some kind of goodbye?" he asks.

I take a deep breath.

"Because Lana is your girlfriend, and she's my friend. We shouldn't be having talks like this or spending time together alone, not when . . ." I don't finish my sentence, but it's written in my voice. *Not when we've possibly just crossed the boundaries of friendship into something else.*

He nods quickly.

"I get it. You're right."

I'll be good, I'll close the door before it can open all the way—but I won't forget the way he made me feel. I'll let the glow of his words carry me, keep me warm, and replenish me in the days to come.

And that will have to be enough.

It's the first Saturday since Chace died, and all of us at Oyster Bay Prep wear the same expression of uncertainty. We're grasping at loose ends, unsure of what to do with two days of free time when there's only grief and fear to fill them. The concept of "the weekend" has lost all meaning in the shadow of his death. There won't be the usual fall Saturday soccer game, followed by an after-party on the field when Chace inevitably leads our team to a win. You won't find the typical cluster of friends squeezed into one dorm room, talking and laughing over music while sneaking sips from a bottle of wine one of us smuggled from home. The weekend Halloween festivities have all been canceled. There's nothing for us to do but wander the campus aimlessly, or shut ourselves in our dorm rooms to wait—for an arrest, or for life to resume some semblance of normalcy.

Detective Kimble won't let any of us leave town while we're still under investigation, so those of us close to home can't even spend a night in the comfort of our childhood bedrooms. We're all equally trapped. Not even my powerful mother could get permission for me to spend the weekend in DC, though she did manage to get Headmaster Higgins to concede to letting me out for an off-campus lunch. The thought of sitting across from Mom at a stuffy hotel restaurant wouldn't normally cheer me up, but today it's just what I need.

I dress quickly, throwing together an all-black outfit, while Stephanie lazes about on the bed.

"I wish I could go with you," she says. "I don't know what to do with myself here."

"Yeah, but you need permission from Higgins to go anywhere," I remind her. And the truth is I'm glad she can't come. There are things I need to ask my mom about, things I don't want Stephanie to hear.

I make my way down to the eerily quiet quad, which would ordinarily be teeming with students, and hike through the campus grounds until I hear the whoosh of noise. The paparazzi and nosy spectators camped outside the entrance gates have just spotted me. But before I can react, a black SUV pulls up. My mom's security officer, Thompson, jumps out of the car and opens Mom's door.

"Clear a path for the congresswoman!" he bellows. I

suppress an inappropriate urge to laugh as Mom cuts through the crowd to get to me and Thompson holds back the over-zealous spectators.

"You know what to say to their questions," Mom murmurs into my ear, wrapping me in a hug.

She grips my hand, and together we walk through the gates and into the din of shouted questions.

"Lana, what happened to your boyfriend?" "What do you have to say to the claims about Chace Porter and Nicole Morgan?" "Lana, was there trouble in paradise between you and Chace?" "Do you think Nicole killed him?" "Tell us, what happened?"

The rapid-fire questions blend into each other, drowning me in noise. But then Mom gives me a gentle nudge, and I remember what to say. I take a deep breath and turn to face the hungry crowd.

"I am a girlfriend in mourning. I don't know anything about the investigation. All I know is that the boy I loved is gone. Please grant me my privacy during this time." My voice is quiet, but strong enough to silence them. And in the brief moment before their shouts start up again, Mom and I dash through the camera flashes into the waiting SUV.

"I'm proud of you, mija," Mom tells me once we're safely ensconced in the backseat.

"It was almost all true," I reply.

"I know." She pats my hand soothingly, and it occurs to me that out of all the weeks in my seventeen-year-old life, this one has shown my mom in her most maternal light, starting from the moment she heard the news and flew to my side. I guess it just takes a high-profile crisis to bring that out in her.

"You know I'd do anything for you, right, Lana?" she says, as if reading my mind.

"I know. Thanks, Mom."

"You can tell me anything." She peers carefully into my eyes. "I won't be angry."

I shift uncomfortably in my seat. What is she getting at?

"I don't have anything to say."

After stepping into the hotel restaurant and seeing all the heads swivel in our direction, my mom and I quickly duck out.

"Room service," we both agree.

Upstairs in her suite, with its cheerful white-and-Tiffany-blue color scheme, I feel myself begin to relax, the tight fist of dread loosening its grip on me. Cocooned in this hotel room, away from the horror at Oyster Bay, I can almost pretend I'm on some sort of vacation—and that when I return, it won't be to a school crawling with police and paparazzi.

"I got you a few new things," Mom says as she picks up the phone to dial room service. "They're in the closet."

"Oh, thanks."

It's probably more black clothing. Two days after Chace died, Mom was flicking through my dorm room armoire, taking note of how few mourning-appropriate outfits I had. I don't know how she remembered to think of clothing at a time like this, but I shouldn't be surprised. This is my mother, after all—the same person *Glamour* and *Latina* magazines both refer to as "Superwoman."

While Mom calls in our order, I open the closet doors. It's one of the more spacious hotel closets I've seen, and it takes me a minute to find the three hangers covered in plastic. Sure enough, I find one black dress and two black tops underneath.

I return the new clothes to their hangers, my nausea resurfacing. I never imagined I'd be dressed in black because of him.

As I turn to leave the closet, my eyes catch a duffel bag peeking out from the top shelf. I stop short, recognizing the signature Henri Bendel stripes. That's *my* bag—the one I apparently didn't even realize was missing. Why on planet earth would my mom run off with it?

I hear Mom switch on the TV to her favorite talking-heads political newscast, and I know I can bank on at least a few minutes of privacy while she's distracted. I gently close the closet door and grab a hanger, standing on my tiptoes and using the hanger to pull the bag to the edge of the shelf. It falls into my arms, the tag with my monogrammed initials scratching my wrist. Mom definitely took this out of my dorm—but *why?*

I unzip the bag, and my hands begin to tremble at the sight of the soft silver fabric inside. The blood rushes to my head. My legs buckle underneath me, a silent scream lodging in my throat.

It's my sweater—the Kate Spade one I wore to the party last weekend, the last night I saw Chace. Its sleeves are caked in dried blood.

"Mom!" I try to shout, but my voice is strangled. *"Mom."*

My head is spinning, showing me images of things that can't be right, can't be real. As my mother approaches the closet, I point a shaky finger at the sweater.

"What is this?" I whisper. "Why do you have it?"

Mom lunges toward my duffel bag, stuffing the sweater back inside and zipping it closed before turning to face me.

"I found it in your dorm," she finally answers, and lets out a long exhale. "It was when I was looking for something appropriate for you to wear to the funeral. Thank God I got to it before Detective Kimble did."

I shake my head, her words failing to make any sense. It's as though I've entered an absurdist play and everyone knows the lines but me.

"But I didn't—why is there blood—?"

And then snippets of memory engulf me.

Ryan Wyatt is standing behind the kitchen counter at Tyler Hemming's party, pouring drinks into plastic cups like some kind of amateur bartender. I can't find Chace anywhere, and my frustration is mounting when I finally spot him—talking in a corner with her. But that can't be right. Whatever little thing they had is over. She told him herself that she never wanted to speak to him again.

But there they are now, unaware they're being watched. He says something that makes her smile and she looks like a sad clown, smiling with that teardrop scar on her cheek.

I blink and the scene changes.

It's hours later, past midnight, and the party is over. Everyone is gone, everyone but me and . . . Ryan? Yes, Ryan Wyatt. We're outside, arguing about something. I'm gesturing wildly, showing him the blood on my sweater.

"What did you do, Lana?" I hear him slur. He's drunk, too.

I dig my fingernails into the inside of my wrist, and the memory fades. My eyes snap open.

"I didn't kill him," I tell Mom, but the words aren't as convincing as they once were. "I don't remember everything from that night, but I—I couldn't have. I was mad, but not enough to . . ." I can't finish the sentence.

"Listen to me, Lana," Mom says, lowering her voice. "Whatever did or didn't happen, I choose to believe it wasn't your fault. But that night is over. There's no bringing Chace back. What we need to focus on now is protecting your future, and the future of our family."

"But what if it was my fault?" I whisper. "How could you protect me then?"

"Because you're my daughter," Mom says firmly. "And besides, you just said you didn't do it. So you didn't."

I swallow hard, a lump burning in my throat.

"Do the detectives even have anything on Nicole? Or was that all just you fanning the flames?"

Mom gives me a disapproving look.

"Really, mija. Even I don't have the kind of power to create a suspect. Obviously Detective Kimble has her eye on Nicole for her own reasons."

Except I know she's wrong. I've heard stories about my mom twisting the president's actual arm. What's a small-town detective in comparison?

"Just a few more washes and the stains will be gone," Mom continues, nodding at the duffel bag. "It's not safe to throw it out, what with the cops searching the garbage, but I can send it through the incinerator once I get back to DC."

I stare at her, wondering how she can be so calm and calculating. Has she done this sort of thing before?

The doorbell rings. Room service is here, jarring us out of one reality and into another. My mom smooths her hair and heads to the door while I remain frozen in place. And then a thought hits me.

Ryan saw me wearing the bloodied sweater the night Chace died. If he thought I killed his friend, he wouldn't have wasted a minute before calling the cops on me. So then . . . he must have an explanation for the blood on my hands.

I snatch my phone from my pocket, and quickly type Ryan's name into the text window.

We need to talk.

"Hey, can I talk to you about something?"

I glance up from the sheet music in my lap. Lana is propped up on her bed opposite mine, methodically applying bright red polish to her toenails. She doesn't meet my eyes.

"Of course," I reply. "What is it?"

"Have you noticed anything off about Chace?"

The question takes me aback.

"What do you mean, off?" I push my sheet music away with my foot, as if Lana might see the song title and know what it means, who it's from. But it's only a song. I haven't done anything wrong—have I?

Lana lets out a frustrated sigh.

"I don't know. Something is just different. In the beginning he was all about me, and now it seems like . . ." Her voice lowers. "Like his heart isn't in it anymore. Which is crazy, I know. But that's how it feels."

My cheeks grow hot, and I pray I'm not turning visibly red. I've stayed true to my word, I haven't spent any time alone with Chace since our last conversation, but I've felt it every time we've been near each other in group settings. There's an electric charge between us, an intrinsic pull, and I recognize now that this is what I was so frightened of when he first approached me, before I pushed him toward Lana. I was afraid of feeling too much.

"Hello?" Lana waves a hand in front of my face. "Did you hear me?"

"Sorry!" I say, with a stab of guilt. "I was just . . . trying to remember if I've noticed Chace acting weird. But I don't think you have anything to worry about. If he's the one you're supposed to be with, nothing will keep you two apart."

Are those words for Lana's benefit or my own? I look into her picture-perfect face, wondering what I would do if they broke up. Would I go out with Chace if he still wanted me? Am I really the kind of person who could hurt my friend?

"Well, I hope you're right," Lana says, blowing on her nails. "Anyway, don't mention this conversation to anyone, okay?"

"Of course not." The guilt presses against my stomach once again, and I tell myself it's okay, I'll keep doing the right thing. I'll continue staying away from him, even if they do break up.

"I'm really bummed we can't go to your showcase tomorrow," Lana says, changing the subject. "I can't miss tutoring if I have any hope of passing Monday's chemistry test, but believe me, I would much rather be in the city watching you."

"Don't worry," I tell her. "I totally get it."

"Do you have anyone else coming?"

"Just my mom. The school orchestra has their own rehearsal, so Brianne and the others won't be able to make it. It's probably for the best, though," I admit. "I mean, Brianne was sweet about it when I finally told her I got into the showcase, but . . . things have felt kind of awkward since then."

"You've risen above her socially, too," Lana says bluntly. "You're popular-adjacent now."

I laugh, but I feel a twinge of discomfort. I'm not supposed to be this girl—the kind of girl who makes Brianne jealous, who attracts Lana's boyfriend.

Except for the moments I'm onstage, I'm meant to be on the sidelines. That's how it's always been.

APRIL 3, 2016

I peek through the curtain backstage at David Geffen Hall, the familiar preshow nerves setting in. Yet there's nothing familiar about a stage this grand. I can't even make out who's who in the mass of faces under the blinding bright lights; all

I can see is that the theater is packed. They're all here for us, to witness "the next generation of musical greats," as the poster outside says. Scouts from Juilliard are supposedly in attendance, along with reporters from the *New York Times*'s performing arts beat. I'm beginning to feel faint.

"You got this," Damien says, squeezing my shoulder as he passes by.

I let go of the curtain, following him to our seats in the strings section.

"How is it that you don't seem nervous at all?" I ask. "I feel like I might throw up."

"Oh, I still have the about-to-throw-up feeling," Damien says with a wink. "You just get used to it over time. And the high once you're onstage and the waiting is all over makes it completely worth it."

"That's true."

I watch as the rest of the musicians take their seats on the stage, all of us in standby mode until the curtain lifts. And then we hear the thunder of applause as our conductor takes the stage. The moment is almost here. I can hear my heartbeat echoing in my ears.

"Over the past month, it has been my pleasure to work with twelve of the finest young musicians in the country," Franz Lindgren says, his voice booming through the theater. "I'm delighted to present the 2016 New York Philharmonic Contemporary Youth Showcase!"

The curtain rises. Applause and whistles fill the air. I

glance at Damien and my fellow string players, my nerves building, palms growing sweaty. This is the one day I have to be perfect, the one time I can't afford a single mistake. Thankfully, our opening number is "Summertime," the one I know best. But the beginning notes are all on me.

I blink in the bright lights, my legs trembling, waiting for the conductor's cue. As he raises his baton, I lift my bow to the strings. *This is what I was meant to do. It's my turn.*

I close my eyes and begin to play, letting my favorite melody lift me up, until I no longer see the lights or the seats or the hundreds of faces in the audience. I'm in another world, one whose only inhabitants are me and the musicians on this stage, and this glorious sound.

The roar of applause after the final note jars me back to reality. And now, I can look out at the audience without feeling shaky from nerves. I spot Mom in the third row, beaming with pride, and I smile back at her. We move into Brahms's Hungarian Dance no. 1 in G Minor, and I let myself relax, have fun with the intricate string work, even though it's one of my trickiest numbers. It's a trio piece, with just me, Damien, and the pianist attempting to do justice to Brahms. And from the light in their eyes as we finish, I can tell we nailed it.

And then, just as I'm hitting my stride, something pulls my focus. A latecomer is walking down the aisle of the theater, and there's something about his walk, his build, his profile as he turns to slide into a seat. It's Chace. And he's come right at the moment when I'm about to play his song. My hand stumbles, my bow drops into my lap. I bend down to pick it up, my cheeks burning with humiliation. I've never dropped a bow onstage before. Damien shoots me a look, and I can read his expression. *What the hell?*

I shouldn't look at Chace; it'll distract me even more. But he's smiling, his expression urging me on. I close my eyes, forcing myself to shake off my slipup and focus on the song. When Mr. Lindgren heard me playing it before rehearsal, he insisted on including it in the showcase as our jazz piece. I must have been good then—and I'll be even better now.

> *"Tomorrow is my turn,*
> *No more doubts, no more fears."*

I whisper the words as my bow flies across the strings, making the minor chords and blue notes dance. Knowing he's watching might have thrown me off before, but it fuels me now, giving my performance a new fire. I leap up from the formal orchestra chair and my body moves to the beat, losing myself in it, as the drums, piano, and horns play behind me.

> *"And my only concern for tomorrow*
> *Is my turn."*

After the last long, wailing note, I can't resist raising my violin in the air, beaming upward, where that performance surely came from. And then the audience jumps to its feet. It's the first standing ovation of the night.

I find Chace's eyes in the crowd. They're glimmering.

"Thank you," I whisper. He can't hear me, I know. But I hope he can read my lips.

. . .

Backstage, we shake off our proper onstage personas and turn wild, unleashing the joyful beasts born out of all the applause. We jump up and down, we scream and cheer, we throw our arms around fellow musicians whom we've maybe only said two words to outside of rehearsals.

"To the best young players in the country!" Damien declares, holding up his bottle of Evian.

"To us!" we cry, clinking plastic water bottles.

Franz LIndgren throws open the doors to the backstage greenroom.

"I don't say this often, but *wundervoll!*" he exclaims, sweeping into the room with a rare smile. "You were marvelous." Is it my imagination, or is the conductor looking directly at me when he says those words?

"Your public awaits," he continues, nodding at the theater doors. "Enjoy this victory, and remember: keep up the good work and you just might find a regular home for yourself here at Lincoln Center when you graduate."

The thought sends shivers of excitement through me. I can see that life so clearly in my mind: My own one-bedroom in the city, walking distance from Juilliard. My music stand permanently set on this stage, ready for me to return, night after night, to play. And Chace Porter, sitting in the front row or waiting backstage, but always near.

I blink rapidly. *Where did that come from?* How did he enter my daydream, as seamlessly as though he's been there all along? What kind of person envisions her friend's boyfriend in her own future? I shake my head to rid the image from my mind. *Not me.*

The crowd backstage is thinning out now, my fellow musicians making their entrance into the theater to greet the audience. I follow them through the stage door and out into the orchestra pit.

"That's her, the violinist!" "Nicole Morgan!"

I glance around me in a slight shock, as well-dressed men and women line up to shake my hand or ask for a picture. In this heady moment, all I'm capable of is a repeated mumble of "Thank you." Out of the corner of my eye, I see the people I'm dying to talk to the most. My mother, of course, a proud smile brightening her face as she films my audience encounter on her iPhone. And Chace, standing in the back, away from the lights but still capturing my focus. *Why is he here?*

"Miss Morgan, I'm Professor Portman from Juilliard's Music Division."

My head snaps up.

"Juilliard?" I echo, taking in the woman's sharp features, framed by wire-rimmed glasses.

"Yes." Her face relaxes into a smile. "I have to say, I was very impressed tonight. You shine when playing both classical and contemporary music, which is a rare gift for a violinist. Will you be applying to Juilliard?"

"Of—of course!" I stammer. "It's my dream."

"Consider it a dream very likely to come true." She slips a card into my hand. "My information is all there. You can have your parents contact me. If your performance remains at this standard, we will certainly have a place for you in the String Department."

I have to grip the back of a chair to keep from falling over at this dizzying news. Professor Portman catches the eye of my mom, who waves at me while continuing to film with a giant grin.

"Is that your mother?" she asks.

I nod.

"I'd love to speak with her."

"Professor Portman," I call out, as she turns in her direction. "Thank you so much."

I watch, pinching myself, as the Juilliard professor approaches Mom. And then, as they begin to talk, I make my way up the aisle of the theater to where he stands.

"I knew you would be amazing," Chace says. "But you were even better."

"Thank you for giving me that song." I look up into his blue-gray eyes. "And thank you for coming. I don't know why, but I . . . I played better once I saw you here."

The words feel like too big of an admission after I say them, and my cheeks blaze with guilt. I try to focus my attention on Mom and Professor Portman, who appear engrossed in conversation down at the foot of the stage.

"I can't believe tonight happened," I marvel. "I mean, is this real life?"

Chace laughs softly.

"It most definitely is."

"Does Lana know you're here?" I blurt out.

He shakes his head.

"Why are you here, Chace?" I whisper.

He lets out a long exhale.

"I didn't want to miss it. And I . . ."

"What?"

"Do you think we could go back to when we first met?" He takes a step closer. "And this time, make a different choice?"

I'm on the verge of losing my balance yet again. I stumble into one of the velvet-backed audience chairs, and Chace takes the seat beside me.

"That would mean you breaking up with Lana." I stare down at the carpeted floor. "It would mean her never speaking to me again."

"That part will suck for all of us, I know. But I also know Lana will get over it," he says. "She's a strong girl who can have her pick of guys."

"But you're the one she wants."

He gently tilts my chin toward his face. I suck in my breath.

"And you're the one I want," he whispers. "Do you see my problem?"

"Why?" I ask. "Why me, when you can have her?"

His hand drops to his lap. He leans back in his chair, eyes up to the ceiling.

"Because you're fresh air," he says. "Being around you, hearing your music and listening to you talk, watching you smile . . . it makes me forget all the bad in the world."

I don't trust myself to speak. I've never heard words like that before, and they're turning me inside out, urging me to let go, to let myself fall.

"What about you?" he asks. "Do you think you could one day feel the same?"

"I'm already starting to." I close my eyes, half afraid to meet his. "There were so many things I imagined happening today, but the one thing I didn't dare to envision, the biggest surprise, was you. And I'm . . . I'm glad you're here."

Chace breaks into a smile, dimples appearing on each of his cheeks. I long to reach out and touch them, but I keep my hands in my lap.

"If we're going to—to consider talking to Lana and really do this, I would need to know the truth," I tell him. "About your secret trips to Brooklyn."

His smile fades, but he nods resolutely.

"I know. And I understand it might change your mind."

Before I can respond, Mom comes running up the aisle, clearly oblivious to the conversation taking place.

"Darling, you did it!" She pulls me out of my chair, nearly clobbering me in a bear hug. "They want you at Juilliard! The professor even said you're a top candidate for a *full* scholarship! I'm so proud of you, sweetie."

"Thanks, Mom. *We* did it," I tell her, before turning toward Chace. "This is my friend from school, Chace Porter."

"It's a pleasure to meet you, ma'am," he greets her. "You should be incredibly proud."

Mom raises an eyebrow at me, and I can practically hear her thoughts.

"It's *very* nice to meet you," she says, shaking his hand and flashing me a grin.

"If you don't already have plans, would it be all right if I take Nicole out to celebrate?" he asks. "I'll make sure to get us both back to Oyster Bay before curfew."

Mom cocks her head to the side, considering, but I know the answer is going to be yes. She's never seen me with a boy before—and she's probably as curious as I am to know how this story will unfold.

"All right." She glances down at her watch. "It's six o'clock now, so that gives you just under three hours to catch the train. You'll be sure to make it?"

"I promise," I tell her, my heartbeat picking up speed at the thought of the hours ahead—with Chace.

18

LANA

remember when I first had an inkling of what was going on. It was right here on the soccer field, last April. Soccer season was over, but that particular Saturday was a charity game between Oyster Bay Prep and Houghton Academy—otherwise known as Oyster Bay's off-season excuse to flaunt Chace's athletic prowess. I was seated in the front row of the bleachers, of course, flanked by Kara, Stephanie—and Nicole.

I kick my shoes into the dirt as I walk toward the bleachers now, my mind and body reliving that day six months ago. It was always such a rush watching Chace play. He was so much faster than everyone else; he was more wind than human when he took to the field. I loved the way his muscles flexed as he moved, how his tanned skin glistened under the sun. I loved the fierce concentration on his face as he commandeered the ball, and more than anything I loved the deafening roar when he scored goal after goal. Sometimes he would even look at me after each of those victories, and my whole body swelled with pride.

But on that April day, he made a mistake. He actually looked at *her* after scoring a goal. Her cheeks blushed bright pink, and I felt my stomach turn to ice.

It couldn't have been on purpose. That's what I told myself. He meant to look at me, and she was sitting so close. Except, he didn't glance my way for the rest of the game.

After Oyster Bay's win, we rushed the field, as we always do. I threw my arms around Chace, and though he hugged me back, there was no kiss. I pretended everything was fine, of course. While he made his rounds, fist-bumping his teammates and thanking everyone lining up to congratulate him, I talked and joked loudly with Kara and Stephanie like nothing was wrong—because of course nothing was, I was only being paranoid. Still, I ignored Nicole, pretending she wasn't there. And then one minute I looked up, and she wasn't.

Neither was Chace.

They were off to the side, engrossed in a conversation about who-knows-what, Chace looking down at her with a smile that made my heart plummet. Seeing the happiness on both of their faces was like standing beneath the sun, lifting my face to its rays, and yet cut off from feeling any of its warmth. I must have known it then. The two of them, my boyfriend and my roommate, were making the unthinkable choice of cutting *me* off from the light.

Ryan Wyatt had sidled up to me while I watched them, and he followed my gaze.

"They sure look happy, don't they?" he remarked with a patronizing smile.

I turned to shoot him a furious glare. How *dare* he talk like that about my boyfriend and my roommate, as if the two of them were even a "they" in the first place? I may have been neutral on Ryan before, but in that moment, my feelings turned to hate.

"You wanted to see me?"

I turn around, jolted from my memory by the sound of Ryan's present-day voice. His hair is an uncombed mess, his eyes rimmed with dark circles.

"You look terrible," I remark.

"Thanks," he says drily. "So what's this about? I'm not usually your choice of people to hang out with."

I take a deep breath. I have no choice but to dive in.

"The party," I answer. "I remember us talking that night. I was upset. Do you know why?"

I sink into a seat on the bleachers, wrapping my arms around my knees. Ryan sits beside me.

"Is this a trick question?" he asks.

"No, I just—I need to know what we said."

"I was drunk that night, too, I don't—" Ryan starts to rebuff me, when suddenly a light flashes in his eyes. "Wait. I think I know what you're talking about."

He sounds amazed, as though recalling our conversation is some kind of accomplishment.

"You're the reason it's been so impossible to remember that night," I snap at him. "You and your screwed-up drinks."

He ignores me, squinting at a point far in the distance.

"You were griping to me about Chace. You guys had just had a fight. I asked you about the blood on your wrist, and you said it was an accident. But then . . ." He clears his throat, his voice sharpening. "You told me it wouldn't surprise you if Chace was responsible for Nicole's scar."

I stare at Ryan.

"I didn't mean it."

"We were all drunk," Ryan replies. "I didn't read into anything you said."

"Why haven't you told the cops?" I ask, my voice barely above a whisper. "If he and I got into that kind of a fight—"

I stop mid-sentence as another image floods my mind.

Chace and I are in the woods. He stands a few feet away from me, shaking his head as I yell at him, angry, hot tears rolling down my cheeks. He opens his mouth and words come out that sting and burn, so much that I grab the nearest rock I can find and fling it at him. It hits him square in the forehead. Blood trickles down.

"Oh God!" I yelp. I'll be in real trouble now, when all I wanted was for him to feel a fraction of the hurt he caused me. I run to

Chace and press the sleeve of my sweater to his forehead, trying to stanch the bleeding, but he pushes me away.

"Just get out of here, Lana. Leave me alone."

"He was alive and talking to me when I left," I blurt out.

"I know. That's why there was no point in me telling the cops about the fight. That, and the fact that I need to keep a low profile. Already, the cops are all up in my business just because Chace and I were such good friends. If they knew I'm the one who made the drinks—" He stops short, panic in his eyes as he looks at me. "You're not going to tell, are you?"

But I'm barely listening. I'm relishing my relief, the tension seeping out of my body like air from a pricked balloon. Until a thought occurs to me.

Just because he was alive when I left the woods—doesn't mean that it's not my fault he's dead.

"Lana." Ryan elbows me. "What do you say? Are we going to look out for each other in this?"

The thought of aligning myself with Ryan makes me cringe, but I have no choice. I can't afford to make an enemy of him, not when he knows about the fight.

"Fine. But this doesn't make us buddies."

19

NICOLE
APRIL 3, 2016

The train stops at Atlantic Terminal in Brooklyn, and this time I get out alongside Chace. He reaches for my hand as we step off the platform, and although my mind protests that we should wait until we've talked to Lana, I lose my resolve at his touch. His fingers interlace with mine as if they've done so countless times before, and my breath catches in my throat. This can't be anything illicit or wrong, not when it feels so natural—like everything is in the right place.

"I haven't told anyone this before. Only my parents know," Chace begins, lowering his voice as we cross the street. I can tell he's nervous, and I give his hand a gentle squeeze.

"A year ago, I found out something about my dad. My

parents had been fighting a lot, and when I asked questions, they always just blamed it on the stress of keeping his seat in Congress. I was pissed at him for creating such a crappy environment at home—like, was any job really worth it? And then one day I had an idea. Back in elementary school, he would pick me up and take me to Wiseguy Pizza once a week for father-son time. That was our thing, before he got elected." Chace smiles sadly. "So I thought, hey, why not surprise him at the office with a pie from Wiseguy, remind him of old times, and maybe cheer him out of his funk?"

"That's really sweet of you," I tell him, though I have a feeling this story doesn't end well.

"So I did." Chace grits his teeth. "And when I walked in, I found him making out with one of his staffers, Lucy Jensen. The two of them were half dressed. *Lucy,* who had been over to our house with her husband and kids plenty of times, and who always pretended to be my mom's friend. I lost it when I saw them together."

I shudder.

"I can't even imagine. That must have been horrible."

We pass the massive Barclays Center arena and turn the corner to a residential street, lined with handsome brownstone homes.

"I wanted to get back at my dad, and while he and Lucy were sucking face, I grabbed his spare car keys off a shelf in his office, where I knew he kept them. When they finally noticed me in the room, they both freaked out, and I took off while they started throwing clothes back on. I went down to the office parking garage. This was sophomore year, so I didn't even have a driver's license yet, but I was so mad, I didn't care. I took my dad's Audi." Chace stares down at the gray sidewalk. "I drove it to the Jensen house downtown. I don't know what I was thinking, maybe that I'd go tell Mr. Jensen what my dad and his wife were up to? Who knows—clearly I *wasn't* thinking. I was in this blind rage, until I felt my car hit something."

Chace stops in his tracks, and I follow his gaze. We're staring up at a brownstone, identical to all the rest except in this one there's a boy in the window, leaning on a cane as he hobbles toward the kitchen table.

"I should have called 911, but I called my dad first. And he told me to go." Chace's voice is barely above a whisper. "He said he would come take care of it, that everything would be okay as long as I drove straight home and never said a word about this to anyone."

I shake my head, my stomach in knots.

"And that's what you did?"

"Yes." Chace's voice breaks. "Dad sent his right-hand assistant to the scene, and that's how we found out that the thing I hit was a person. Ten-year-old Brady Jensen, the same age as my little brother, Teddy."

I cover my mouth with my hand.

"Is he . . . ?"

"Alive? Yes, thank God." Chace lets out a long exhale.

"Dad paid for every surgery, but he also paid for something else. See, Lucy Jensen knew it was me. She saw me walk in on them, and she was with my dad right after, when they came looking for me and discovered the car was gone. And I was desperate to tell the truth—it was eating away at me, the need to say I was sorry. But my parents sat me down and said it wasn't just me I'd be sacrificing if I told the truth. My dad's bid for reelection would never survive his son confessing to a hit-and-run."

"So what happened?"

"I don't know how much money he threw at them, but it must have been a lot. And I'm guessing the Jensens had no desire for the truth to get out, either, since that would expose Lucy's dirty secret. So the next thing I knew, their older son, Brady's brother, Justin, came forward and told the police it was him. He had a whole story prepared about how he'd been practicing for his license test, when he lost control of the car and panicked once he realized what he'd done." Chace swallows hard. "I never saw Justin again."

"What? He went to jail?" I ask in horror.

"No, but he did go to juvie. I don't think anyone expected anything to happen to him, since it was supposedly a family matter, but the state doesn't treat hit-and-runs lightly, no matter who's involved. Especially when they did a drug test and found weed in Justin's system. I guess they thought they could make an example of him." Chace rakes his hand through his hair, and for the first time I notice the sadness behind his blue-gray eyes. It was always there—I just never put my finger on it until now.

"I don't understand why Justin would take the fall," I say, shaking my head. "I mean, I can sort of understand adults being influenced by money, but a kid our age?"

Chace takes a deep breath.

"Justin caused his parents more than a few headaches over the years, and I know he felt bad about it as he got older. He was a good guy, but he was constantly blowing off school and getting high. My dad once told me Lucy had to take off work practically every other week for parent-teacher meetings. My guess is, Justin's parents convinced him that by taking the fall and earning them my dad's bribe money . . . he'd be making it up to them in some way."

I stare at Chace, finding it impossible to believe that the golden boy standing in front of me, whose every interaction with me pulls at my heart, is only here because another boy took his place in a cell. I take a gulp of air.

"Is he . . . out?"

"My parents told me it was a short sentence, so I think he's out now. Although, who knows if they were just trying to calm me down when they said that. They considered me a ticking time bomb, I was so racked with guilt and anxious to tell the truth. So they sent me away to Oyster Bay Prep." Chace meets my eyes for the first time. "I guess that's the only thing I can't be mad at them for—that they brought me here."

My thoughts are running all over the place, and I struggle to focus them.

"What about Brady? Is he okay?"

Chace gazes up at the brownstone in front of us.

"I've been following his recovery every day since the accident. I found out that he was moved to New York to be treated by the best physical therapist on the East Coast, and that he was living at his aunt and uncle's place in Brooklyn. I had to see him, to know for myself that he really was getting better. So I became a volunteer at Rusk Institute of Rehabilitation Medicine, and I offered to help Brady with his exercises on the weekends."

"That's him," I say, realization dawning as I stare at the shadow of the boy in the window.

"Yeah. He's doing so well." Chace smiles slightly. "He'll finally be rid of the cane soon. And we've become buddies, Brady and I."

"But what does his family say about you being the volunteer? I mean, they obviously know the truth."

"His aunt and uncle don't know me, Lucy never told them the real story, and I use a different name when I'm here," Chace admits. "But you don't know how much I want to tell the truth. The fact that Brady's getting better doesn't alleviate any responsibility I feel. And it's not fair that I get to have the whole world ahead of me while Justin is who-knows-where, with a record to his name."

"I need to sit down," I blurt out.

Chace nods, leading the way to a coffee shop at the end of the block. I sink into a seat at a corner table, my mind still digesting everything as Chace orders for us.

"I'm sorry," he says, returning with two steaming mugs of coffee. "This was your big day. I feel like I put a major damper on it with my story."

"No. I'm glad you told me."

He tries to smile, but his expression is filled with sorrow.

"Now do you see why I thought you might feel differently about me after hearing this?"

"Yes. But the funny thing is . . . I don't."

I tentatively reach across the table and place my hand over his. The electric charge is still there, sending my stomach swooping, but now there's something deeper beneath it.

"I see someone who made a mistake, but is doing everything he can to make it right, even when it means going against his parents. I see someone brave enough to be honest."

His eyes fill with gratitude as he gazes at me.

"And when I do tell the truth . . ."

"You'll have me by your side," I tell him. "I promise."

• • •

We sit beside each other on the train back to Oyster Bay, both quiet as we watch the nighttime scenery fly past. Everything we've shared and spoken over the past few hours seems to have turned us shy as the train hurtles back to Long Island.

Will he regret confiding in me? I wonder. *Will we both regret what we're about to confess to Lana?*

The train speeds past a sharp turn, and my body slams against Chace's.

"Sorry!" I exclaim, my face reddening.

He wraps a gentle arm around me.

"You okay?"

I glance up at him. Our faces are so close. I can feel his warm breath against my cheek. My heartbeat quickens.

"Yes."

Our eyes remain locked. I know we both ache for the same thing—his lips on mine. But our first kiss can't happen behind Lana's back. I lower my head away from his, resting it on his shoulder.

From the back row of the train car comes the sound of an acoustic guitar. I turn around in my seat. A twentysomething, scruffy-bearded man is playing, a change cup beside him.

"It's a busker," I tell Chace. He begins to sing.

"Whenever I'm alone with you
You make me feel like I am home again . . ."

"Doesn't Adele sing this?" I hum along.

"It's originally by the Cure," Chace replies.

"You know an awful lot about music for an athlete," I say, looking up at him teasingly. "Where did all that knowledge come from?"

"I guess the fact that I can't sing on key or play an instrument to save my life makes me appreciate those who do," he says with a grin. "I've always been a giant music fan, but mostly for older stuff."

"I like that about you," I tell him.

"And I like everything about you," he murmurs into my hair.

My heart jumps, and I try to control my smile. We fall silent again, Chace's arm still around my shoulder as we listen to the acoustic guitarist at the back of the train.

> *"However far away,*
> *I will always love you . . ."*

20

LANA

There's a trail that leads from the school woodlands straight up a hill, forming a shortcut into the residential streets of Oyster Bay, where Tyler Hemming's family estate sits on a plush pocket of land. I follow the trail now, retracing my steps from the night of the party. The day is turning to dusk, and I quicken my footsteps, anxious to get through my task before night falls.

My iPhone buzzes with a text. It's from Kara.

Where R U? Just saw on the news that there's a lead on Nicole. Something they found on her computer.

I drop my phone back in my purse. I could just turn around and head back to my dorm right now; anyone else would. Who cares what I do or don't remember, when the girl I've hated for months is the obvious suspect and not me? I should just let the police, my mom, and whoever else is pushing the Nicole narrative along sew this case up. But I can't shake the feeling that there's something more, something I need to remember if I'm ever going to recover from this. The problem is, retracing my steps will mean returning to the place I can't stand to see: the woods where we last argued. The place where his body was found.

Still I press on, the occasional bird chirping and the crunching of my shoes against the leaves providing the only soundtrack. And then I see it, out of the corner of my eye—a flash of yellow tape, the word CAUTION screaming its warning in bold black letters.

Now that I'm nearly at the scene of the crime, I want nothing more than to bypass it. I break into a run, keeping my gaze focused on the dirt beneath my feet.

"Lana."

The voice calling my name isn't real. It's only in my head. I keep running, ignoring the stitch in my side.

"Lana."

It's the wind. I'm hearing things, imagining things. But then I feel a pressure against my arm. I spin around, heart in my throat. A bloodcurdling scream escapes my lips.

I can't explain it—but somehow I've run into the very center of the sectioned-off patch of woods, surrounded by the menacing tape. I'm at the beating heart of the crime scene. A familiar figure is standing underneath the weeping willow tree, casually leaning one foot against the tree trunk as he watches me. I fall to my knees in the dirt.

"Chace?" I whisper.

It's impossible. I don't believe in ghosts.

"Lana," he says, and I scramble backward in panic.

"You're not real," I tell him, my voice sounding high-pitched and foreign to my own ears. "You can't hurt me. You're only in my mind."

"Am I?" He smiles slightly, revealing the dimples I used to love. They send a stab of fear through me now. "Even if you're right, if I am only in your mind, I can still be real."

My breath comes out in shallow gulps; I don't know what to think, what to say. When I finally speak, my words come tumbling out in a terrified rush.

"I'm sorry about what happened to you. And I'm sorry about the things I said, and the—the thing with the rock. But I didn't do this to you. You can't blame me."

He just watches me, tapping his finger against his lips, as if weighing my words.

"Why are you even here?" I burst out. "Shouldn't you be, like, on the other side?" I clap my hand over my mouth, cringing. "Wait, I didn't mean it that way, I just mean—"

"You're talking an awful lot like someone who wanted me gone," Chace says roughly.

"No." I shake my head, pleading with my eyes. "I'm not the one you're looking for."

He pauses, and I wonder if he is deliberating whether or not to believe me.

"I can't . . . move on until I know she's okay," he says, looking away. "So if you really want this to be the last time you see me, then you'll help."

I shove my hands into the dirt.

"It's always about Nicole with you. Even after death, it's about her."

Chace steps forward, and I see his reflection ripple against the wind. With a shudder, I realize that if I pressed my hand against his chest, it would plunge straight through. He looks down at me, his expression gentler.

"Lana, you told someone where I was that night after our fight. Who did you tell?"

"What?" I stare blankly up at him. "What are you talking about?"

"You told someone where to find me," he says. "Who was it? *Think.*"

I close my eyes, letting the fragments of memory back in.

Ryan pours drinks into plastic cups. Chace and Nicole huddle in a corner. I'm dragging Chace outside to talk, and the talk becomes a fight. Running back to Tyler's house, I catch sight of Nicole through my tear-blurred vision. I spot her from the back by her sweater, the silver cardigan I gave her for Christmas back when we were still friends—the same one I'm wearing now. She wasn't wearing it earlier tonight, so she must have seen me in the sweater and put hers on just to spite me. She has even more nerve than I thought.

I shudder at the idea of us matching; I should have burned my cardigan months ago. I sprint past her, refusing to meet her eyes as I scream, "Have at him, you bitch!" And then, arriving at Tyler's, I bump smack into Ryan. He tries to calm me down from my alcohol-boosted rage; he offers to walk me back to campus.

I open my eyes, shaking my head in frustration.

"I can't think of anyone besides Nicole and Ryan."

But when I open my eyes, Chace has disappeared.

21

NICOLE

MAY 13, 2016

I lost my nerve so many times after that New York night with Chace. I would look at Lana sleeping in the bed across from mine in our tiny dorm, and affection for her would squeeze itself around my heart, while the voice in my head taunted me: *What right do you have, thinking you can take her boyfriend?* But when I let myself close my eyes and block out the noise, another voice whispered. *You already pushed yourself aside once. Don't make the same mistake twice. Not when this could be real love. She'll understand.*

Maybe it's wishful thinking, but this is the voice that wins in the end. I don't think I've ever really put myself first, but Chace's confidence in us gives me the last push I need. When he asks me to meet the two of them after school on Thursday so we can finally have the talk, my heart answers before my head, and I say yes.

I barely make it through my classes that day. Brianne has to kick my leg twice during History to get me to quit my incessant, jittery foot tapping, and when Mr. Newell calls on me during Algebra, I completely space out, forgetting how to solve an equation I knew perfectly well yesterday. I hide out in the library during lunch, afraid I won't be able to keep my cool at my usual table with her. *If I'm doing the right thing, then why do I feel so guilty?*

I contemplate texting Chace that I've changed my mind, that we should forget the whole thing. But the swift, crushing weight in my chest that follows reminds me that he's worth it. *We're* worth it. I just pray Lana will forgive us.

The last bell finally rings. The hour is here. My stomach flip-flops in unison with my footsteps as I weave through the crowd of students and push through the doors of Academics Hall. I follow the rush of classmates out onto the quad and then change course, heading for the picnic tables beside the tennis courts. They're already sitting there at one of the white wicker tables when I arrive.

"Hi." My voice is like sandpaper as I approach them. I can feel the beads of sweat dotting my brow, and I can't bring myself to look either of them in the eye, afraid I'll reveal too much.

"What are you doing here?" Lana asks, a suspicious edge to her voice.

"I—Chace didn't tell you I was coming?" I stammer, realizing instantly that this wasn't the smartest choice of words.

Lana's eyes narrow into slits.

"What's going on?"

Chace takes a deep breath, focusing his gaze on the table.

"We thought we should tell you this together, since we both care about you so much—"

Lana jumps out of her seat.

"Tell me what?"

She knows. I can see it in her expression. I shut my eyes.

"Nicole and I, we—you mean a lot to both of us, and we never meant to hurt you," Chace begins. "But we . . . have feelings for each other."

A deathly silence follows. And then she starts to laugh, a bitter, hollow sound.

"Great joke, guys. Hysterical."

Chace looks from me to Lana and back again.

"It's not a joke. I'm—I'm sorry."

I finally gather the courage to look at her.

"Lana," I whisper. "If it could have been anyone else . . . but we couldn't help how we felt—"

Her palm strikes my cheek, cutting me off with a shock. I gasp, tears stinging my eyes. Chace jumps in between us, but I hold up my hand to stop him. The last thing Lana needs to see is him defending me.

"It's okay. I deserved that." I wince as I face Lana, her expression twisted with rage. "Lana, please believe me, we haven't gone behind your back or anything. We haven't even kissed."

Lana sputters with angry laughter.

"Wow. Do you actually expect me to thank you for not kissing *my boyfriend*?"

"Lana, don't take this all out on Nicole." Chace steps in. "It's my fault more than hers."

She shakes her head violently.

"How could this even *happen*?"

Chace looks down at the ground.

"When Nicole was doing the Philharmonic concert, I had to be in Brooklyn at the same time. We were on the same train. . . ."

"Brooklyn?" She spits the word. "You told me you were in soccer training. You're a liar *and* a cheat. You're a total cliché." Lana pushes him roughly, her face contorting in pain.

"I wish I'd done everything differently," Chace says, looking between the two of us in desperation. "But, Lana, I couldn't tell you about Brooklyn because my parents—well, it's going to come out soon enough, and honestly, when you hear about the whole thing with the Jensens, you'll be glad you're not with me anymore." He tries to crack a smile, but it comes out looking more like a grimace.

"That's not the point, whatever the hell you're talking about," she snaps. "It should have been *my* choice."

And suddenly, looking in her eyes, I can see what is bothering her the most. It's not the thought of losing Chace. It's the loss of control; it's the idea of losing him to me.

"You're a real dark horse, Nicole," she hisses. "I actually made you my *friend*. I rescued you from having no one but those geeks in orchestra, I *gave* you a social life. It's because of me that you even know Chace. And all along, you were plotting how to stab me in the back and take what's mine."

"No," I plead, tears falling freely now. "It wasn't like that at all."

"Lana, please, let's just talk straight with each other," Chace says gently. "We both know we were pushed together by our parents and their agendas. It was what they wanted, but was it really what you—we—wanted?"

She stares at him.

"Who cares if it started because of them? I thought what we had was real."

Chace hangs his head.

"It was real, I just—"

"You just liked her more," Lana says incredulously. "You do realize every guy in this school will think you've gone completely blind and dense."

He opens his mouth to protest, but I catch his eye, giving him a warning look. The less he says in my favor right now, the better.

"What can we do to make this any . . . any easier?" I ask, my voice barely audible.

Lana crosses her arms over her chest, shooting me a death stare.

"Let's see. You can start by abandoning this whole disgusting plan to betray me. You can stay the hell away from

213

my boyfriend—and from me. And you can get yourself a new roommate, because I never want to see your backstabbing, pathetic face again."

I stumble backward at the force of her words. How could I have been so stupid to think she might actually understand, that there could possibly be a happy ending here?

"I should go," I mumble.

"No, Nicole, wait," Chace calls out, but I shake my head. "Just let me go."

And with that, I break into a run.

• • •

I wait for hours in our dorm, pacing the tiny square footage of the room while hoping against hope that Chace might have somehow succeeded in talking her down. But she never comes back, never responds to a single one of my pleading text messages. I should have known. I was so *stupidly* optimistic in thinking I could actually have this love without losing her. And now looking around our room, littered with her clothes, makeup, and books, I can't feel anything besides the painful lump in my throat, the sick churning in my stomach.

When my phone finally vibrates with a text, it's not from Lana.

I have to see you. Can you meet me under the wooden bridge by the pond? The one before the soccer field. It looks private enough.

Okay,

I type back, a knot forming in my stomach. What is he going to say? What am I going to do?

I step out into the empty dorm corridor. The sounds of silverware scraping against plates, muffled chatter, and occasional bursts of laughter rise up from the Dining Hall downstairs, and it occurs to me that it must be dinner hour. I've completely forgotten.

With everyone in the Dining Hall, no one sees me slip past and out the door. I make my way to the location Chace described, passing the tennis courts and the site of our doomed talk with Lana along the route. At last, I hear the gurgling of water and I know the pond is near. A tall figure stands underneath the bridge, waiting for me. I quicken my footsteps. He turns in my direction, and before I even know what's happening, his arms are around me, my head pressed against his chest. I don't even realize I'm crying until he gently brushes his finger under my eyes, wiping away the tears.

"It's over," he tells me. "I broke up with Lana."

"Was she—was she okay in the end?" I ask, still holding out a sprig of futile hope.

He rakes a hand through his hair, looking at me helplessly.

"Not really. I didn't expect her to be so mad. I handled this all wrong, I know. But I did offer to keep the breakup— and you and me—under wraps until she's ready. That seemed to help a little bit."

I breathe a sigh of relief. I'm not ready to go public any-time soon myself.

Chace tilts my chin up to his face.

"Do you regret this? It's—it's okay if you change your mind."

I look into the pool of his eyes, asking myself the same question. I regret hurting Lana; I would take that back a thousand times if I could. But do I regret me and Chace?

I take a step closer. My hands are tentative as they reach for his shoulders, and he leans down and kisses the inside of my wrist. My body heats up, my legs begin to tremble, as his lips move up my arm, and suddenly I can't wait a moment longer. I lift my face to his. Our bodies are so close, I can hear both of our hearts racing to the same beat. And then our lips meet.

I can't hold back my gasp at the sensation of his kiss. Shivers run up and down my insides as our lips move together, answering every question we might have had. It seems un-fathomable that I've lived without this until now; it's like dis-covering music all over again.

"I don't regret it," I whisper. "I couldn't if I tried."

PART THREE

NICOLE + LANA

"Nicole."

With a gasp, I turn around. I blink rapidly, but his image remains in front of me, those blue-gray eyes gazing down with tenderness.

"It *is* you," I breathe. "When I thought I heard you through my headphones, and outside the school calling to me . . . it was real? But . . . how . . . ?"

He moves toward me and I watch, heart in my throat, as his feet skim above the ground.

"The dead can choose," he says softly. "I chose you."

"Over what?" I whisper.

He gestures upward.

"Passing on. Crossing over. Whatever you want to call it, I won't do it—not until I know you're okay."

The weight in my chest cracks open. The tears come flooding out, burning my eyes and choking my throat. Chace reaches out his hand, and this time he doesn't withdraw. His fingers brush the scar on my cheek. Where his touch used to be warm, today it's a shock of cold. But still, I don't want him to let go.

"I never thought it would take death to bring us back together, but . . ." He shrugs, attempting a smile. "Well, as long as you can forgive me for—for everything."

"Of course I do." I wipe my eyes with the back of my hand. "I'm the one who should apologize. Maybe I could have saved you, if I'd only stayed that night! When Ryan texted me to meet you guys at the party, I can't explain how happy I was. But then I . . . I got scared. I was afraid of something bad happening if we got close again—like what happened with my accident."

"What do you mean?" Chace peers closer at me. "I thought you said you didn't remember that night."

"I don't really, I just remember the feeling I had—that we were both in danger as long as we were together." I swallow hard. "But that's not all I was afraid of. I was scared of how strongly I felt for you, and how much it would hurt to lose you again. I was even afraid of things actually working out—of what it would be like to walk beside you, and have all those eyes and whispers surrounding me and my scar. But now I see how pointless the fears were, and I'm just so sorry I ran out on you after our talk that night. It's killing me, knowing how things might have been different if I'd stayed."

Chace steps closer to me, until our faces are so close I can feel the cold wind of his breath.

"You have nothing to apologize for, Nicole. It's a good thing you left that night. One of us is still alive, and I'm grateful that it's you."

A wave of grief from his words engulfs me. I look up at him, my golden boy, once so solid and full of color, now translucent.

"How does this work? Are you a . . . ?"

"Spirit?" He finishes my sentence. "Must be something like that. There are periods of . . . of nothing, just me and a bright light that I'm fending off. And when I fight hard enough, that's when I find myself here, able to see or communicate with you for moments at a time."

"You shouldn't have to fight," I say, my voice breaking. "You should be at peace."

"How can I be at peace when I still don't know who killed me—and when you might take the fall for it?"

With a chill, I remember my task. The weapon in my backpack.

"Someone planted the—the knife in my room," I tell him. "Do you think if you saw it, you might remember who did this to you?"

A cloud crosses his face, but he holds out his hand.

221

"Show me."

With a shudder, I pull the ziplock bag out of my backpack. His eyes darken as he takes in the blade. He runs his hand over it, and I bite back a scream as the knife glides through his intangible palm—but of course, he draws no blood. Not this time.

"I don't remember." He shakes his head in frustration. "My last memory is the rock."

"What rock?" I press.

He doesn't answer. Instead he takes a step away from the blade in my hands.

"Get rid of it," he says. "You can't be found with this. Bury it someplace where it can't be tracked to you."

"Okay," I whisper, a sick feeling in my stomach. I take a breath, clear my throat.

"I thought about what you said before, about the early days of you and me. Were you talking about our visit to Brooklyn? Do you think this was—I mean, could it be Justin Jensen's revenge or something?"

The idea of Justin—who could still be in juvie, for all we know—risking his family by coming after Chace sounds as far-fetched as anything else I could come up with. But Chace stops still.

"Maybe Justin. Maybe someone else . . ."

His reflection wavers, and I rush forward, trying to hold him in place. But my hands only brush against air.

"Don't go!" I wail. "Stay with me."

But our time is up.

I'm all alone.

Again.

OCTOBER 29, 2016

I know something must be wrong when my phone rings at six a.m. on a Saturday. At first I let it chime on aimlessly, afraid to hear whatever news is on the other end of the line. But on the thirteenth shrill ring, I finally answer.

"Hello?"

"Nicole, it's John Sanford."

In my groggy haze, it takes me a moment to remember who he is. And then, with a wave of dread, it hits me. The lawyer.

"What is it?" I sit up, instantly alert.

"I'm afraid the police found the email you were composing to Chace the same day he died. It's still in your drafts folder."

"What email?" I ask, bewildered. "I didn't write him anything that day."

"You may not have sent it, but the draft is there in black and white. You wrote that you would never forgive Chace, and that you wished he were dead."

The room around me begins to spin. I grip the side of my mattress to keep steady. This isn't happening.

"I *never* wrote that," I tell the lawyer, my voice shaking in my shock. "There must be a mistake. I'll log in to my account and show you—"

"I already saw it, Nicole," Mr. Sanford says heavily. "Detective Kimble sent it to me first as a courtesy."

"But—but that's impossible!" I cry. "I'm telling you, I didn't write that. Someone is setting me up."

I hear him pause.

"That's not the worst of it. Someone turned in your sweater from that night."

"What sweater?" Now it's my head that's spinning. "I didn't lose a sweater."

"It has Chace's blood on it—and hairs that match your DNA. I'm afraid we need to prepare for the worst."

23

LANA

The violent banging at my door shocks me awake. I blink my eyes open, disoriented. The banging continues in earnest and I pull the covers up over my head to block out the noise. If I ignore it, maybe it'll go away.

But then the door to my room is kicked open. I sit bolt upright, a scream lodging in my throat as I see a flash of blue.

It's the cops. What are they doing, why are they here?

"Lana Rivera, you have the right to remain silent," a burly policeman barks at me, brandishing his badge. His partner throws the covers off me, grabbing my elbow and pulling me out of bed.

"Stop! Don't touch me!" I shout.

But now they're pinning my arms behind my back, locking my wrists in handcuffs, not even letting me cover myself up as I stand in pajama shorts and a flimsy tank top.

"Let me go!" I scream. "My mother is a United States Congresswoman. You have to let me *go!*"

"Lana." Someone pokes me in the ribs, then rubs my arm. What the hell? Since when are cops allowed to be so handsy with people? *"Lana!"*

I blink my eyes open. Stephanie is standing over me in pajamas, her hair a tangled mess. I look wildly around the room, but it's just the two of us.

"You were having a nightmare," she tells me. "It was freaky. You just got up like a sleepwalker and started yelling."

"Sorry," I mutter. I fall back into bed, practically wilting with relief. It was a dream—just a dream.

I burrow my head back into the pillow and close my eyes, but all I can see are the panic-inducing images from my nightmare. Looks like sleep is out of the question. I mindlessly reach for my cell, and find it already blinking with a new message. Who would be texting me at two in the morning? Mom, of course.

Turn on the news.

My heartbeat quickens. I jump out of bed and grab my laptop off my desk.

"What are you doing now?" Stephanie groans, but I ignore her, clicking open the Google News window. And there it is, right on the front page: "Nicole Morgan, 'The Girl in the Picture,' Taken into Police Custody in Chace Porter Case."

I stare at the headline, rereading it until the words swim together, turning into gibberish. And then I click the link, pressing play on the video.

The screen reveals Nicole, her scar ghastlier than ever against the paleness of her skin. She shuffles between two cops, who push her up the steps of the Centre Island Police Station. Her arms are locked behind her back, just like mine were in my dream. At the edge of the frame are Nicole's mom and a grim-faced man, the two of them following close behind her. Mrs. Morgan's eyes are watery with tears.

The din of shouting, hungry reporters accompanies the video, and suddenly Nicole stops still, turning toward the camera to face them.

"I didn't do it," she says in that quietly determined voice of hers. "I could *never* have done it. I'm being set up. And I know exactly who—"

My heart is in my throat, waiting for her to finish her sentence, when the man accompanying them jumps in front of her.

"My client has nothing further to say."

So that's her lawyer. I watch as the cops shove Nicole through the doors and she disappears inside, trailed by her mom and the attorney. A wide-eyed NBC News reporter fills the screen.

"For those of you just tuning in, Nicole Morgan, the

student who became infamous on social media this past week as The Girl in the Picture, has been arrested in connection with the murder of Chace Porter. While much was made of the murder weapon being tested for fingerprints on Friday, no match was found on the knife itself. However, an anonymous tip revealed a sweater from the night of Mr. Porter's death, stained with his blood and carrying hairs belonging to Miss Morgan."

I recoil, covering my mouth with my hand.

"Omigod." Stephanie is wide awake now, bolting out of bed to my side. "So she really did it, then? This is insane. . . . Are you okay, Lan?"

I wanted her gone, and now I'm getting my wish. The universe is repaying me for all the hurt she caused, for turning me into this person I no longer recognize. I shouldn't just feel okay. I should feel triumphant.

But instead, I run to the bathroom and vomit into the sink.

• • •

It's all anyone can talk about in the morning, not just at Oyster Bay Prep, but everywhere. "Girl in the Picture" is trending on Twitter, while Nicole's scarred face fills my entire Facebook feed, as practically everyone I know feels the need to post an article about the arrest. Even my mother comments publicly, telling the *Washington Herald:*

"My daughter took Nicole Morgan in as a friend. We even

brought her into our home last year for the holidays. It's been truly terrible for my family to learn that she appears to be responsible for this horrific crime. None of us could have imagined it."

Except you, Mom. You imagined it, all right.

I keep waiting for relief to kick in, but instead all I feel are the walls of my dorm closing in on me, and the fear of another vision from Chace. He'll want me to pay for this. And finally I can't stand it anymore. I pick up the phone.

"Mija." She answers on the first ring. "It's over now."

"Because of you." My voice shakes. "I can't believe you went that far."

She pauses, and then lets out an indignant sputter as she realizes what I meant.

"You think *I* turned in the sweater?"

"Well, who else had it?"

Mom lowers her voice.

"You honestly think I would risk turning in anything of yours? That sweater was Nicole's, and if you don't believe me, come have a look in my closet."

I stare at the phone, more confused than ever.

"She's obviously guilty, and you need to accept it," Mom says crisply. "Honestly, I thought you'd be glad."

She's right, I should be—maybe not *glad* exactly, but at the very least relieved. So why can't I shake the feeling that something seriously shady is going on?

My phone vibrates soon after we hang up, and I'm tempted

to chuck it. But it's not my mom. The name flashing on my screen is Ryan Wyatt.

> This is so insane. I'm freaking out. I never would
> have believed it about Nicole. How are you
> holding up?

That's a surprise. I thought Ryan couldn't care less how I'm doing, but he's also asked when we're out on public display, saying what he thinks he should say to me. Like everyone else. Maybe he feels guilty now, for always being Team Nicole.

> I'm handling it about the same as you.

> Shit. Want to go somewhere and talk? Just feel
> like I need to be around someone who was close
> with Chace too.

I pause, contemplating his offer. I don't particularly want to be around Ryan, or to talk about this with anyone. Then again, is holing up in my dorm and listening to Stephanie's incessant chatter on the topic any better?

> Sure.

• • •

I meet Ryan off campus at the hole-in-the-wall known as Pete's Canteen, the neighborhood's idea of a diner that only serves five things: burgers, tuna melts, milk shakes, fries, and one sad garden salad. Still, now that Headmaster Higgins has loosened her stance enough to let students out within a two-mile radius, at least it gets us off school grounds and onto a quiet backstreet, away from prying spectators and cameras. I spot Ryan already in a booth, and I slide in across from him.

"Hi."

"Hey." He gives me a weak smile in return.

"So." I drum my fingers on the table. "I think it's safe to say we'll never have a worse Halloween weekend than this."

"Tell me about it." He shifts in his seat. "This whole Nicole story has just blown my mind. I mean, can you believe it?"

"You know how I felt about her," I say curtly.

"Yeah." He hangs his head. "I just can't help feeling . . . responsible somehow. You know—because I decided to give the drinks an extra kick. I only wanted to make the night more fun for all of us by getting us buzzed faster, but what if it's my fault that she turned violent?" He looks at me desperately, as if I might have the power to wave away his guilt.

"Well, it was screwed up of you to get everyone so plastered. I'm not going to sugarcoat that, and if I hear about you pulling this crap ever again, I won't hesitate to get you in trouble for it," I warn him. "But. You'll notice no one else killed anyone that night. So it can't have been all you."

Ryan lets out a long exhale.

"Don't worry, I learned my lesson this time. And listen,

there's another reason I wanted to see you. I feel like I owe you an apology for, you know . . . always defending Nicole."

"Thanks," I tell him, trying not to roll my eyes. I knew this is why he wanted to see me.

"Not to be cheesy, but I hope we can be friends now. I feel like we can both help each other through this." Ryan gives me a knowing glance, and I bite back a laugh. He doesn't actually think *now* is an opportune time to hit on me, does he? Guys really are one-track-minded.

"Hey, I'm going to hit the men's room, but feel free to get whatever you want. My treat." He slides his wallet across the table toward me.

Okay, he's definitely hitting on me. No one just hands a girl their wallet unless they want something. *Wishful thinking, Ryan. But I will take a milk shake.*

I'm walking up to the ordering window when I hear the strains of a vaguely familiar voice, talking furiously under her breath. It's coming from the corner booth, the one half hidden by the fake Christmas tree that Pete seems to put up earlier and earlier each year.

"Are you *kidding* me with this?"

There's something about that voice. I turn to look, and . . . it's Brianne, of all people. She's hunched over in her seat, alone in her booth, so riveted by her phone conversation that she doesn't even see me.

"You can actually say that, after everything I've done for you?" She pulls at her dirty-blond hair, her face scrunching up in anguish. I take a slight step closer.

"No, you can't. Not when I risked everything so we—"

A look of shock crosses her face, and she holds the phone in front of her. The person on the other end of the line must have hung up. She slams the phone down onto the table, and as I watch, a strange chill runs through me.

"Hey, did you order—"

I clap my hand over Ryan's mouth to shut him up the second I hear him join me. I've never spared much—if any— thought for Nicole's dull friend, but right now I can't take my eyes off her as she throws a clump of dollar bills onto her table and storms out of the diner. That determined walk of hers reminds me of . . . something. I need to find out what she's up to.

"Come on," I tell him. "We're following her."

"What for?" Ryan looks at me like I've just sprouted two heads.

"I'll explain later, just hurry up and be quiet." I yank his arm, and with a shrug of his shoulders, he falls into step beside me.

Throwing open the diner doors, I spot Brianne several yards ahead, turning into the alley that leads back to school. We trail behind her, me pulling Ryan down with me to duck every time it looks like she might turn around—but I'm only being paranoid. She couldn't be less aware of our presence, crying as she stalks through the alley. Every few moments she lets out a wail of fury, like some kind of wounded animal, and Ryan gives me an indignant look.

"Shouldn't we go help her?" he hisses in my ear. "What the hell are we doing?"

I hold my finger up to silence him as Brianne comes to a halt in front of the Dumpster. She stares from the phone in her hand to the Dumpster before her—and then hurls the phone with all her might, before breaking into a run.

As soon as she's disappeared from view, I turn to Ryan.

"You said you wanted to be friends, right? Well, now's your chance. I need you to dumpster-dive and get me that phone."

24

NICOLE

In my cell, there's only enough room for rumination. I lie on the cold metal floor, forgoing the lumpy yellow cot in favor of something that more closely matches my pathetic state. The girl with the scar, stuck behind bars. No more music, no more future on the Lincoln Center stage.

"*Chace,*" I whisper, angry tears springing to my eyes. "You said you chose me, that you weren't going anywhere till I was okay. So where are you now?"

The sound of skidding footsteps reverberates through the metal floor and stone walls. I sit up.

"Mrs. Porter, you can't just—"

This is my chance. I rush forward, flinging myself at the bars of my cell.

"Mrs. Porter!" I cry.

Chace's mother freezes in place. She stares straight ahead, pretending she didn't hear me, and my heart sinks. But then she turns sharply on her heels, marching to my cell.

"You've got the wrong person!" I cry out. "I didn't do it, they're setting me up—I loved your son, I would never—"

My voice falters as she stops right in front me, her features contorted with rage. She slaps her palms around the bars, covering my hands with hers, digging her sharp fingernails into my skin.

"Was this your idea of revenge?" she hisses.

"What? I told you, I'm innocent!"

She tightens her grip on me.

"Don't you dare lie to me any longer."

That voice. Once again, the sound of it gives me a prickly feeling of familiarity; it sends a wave of dread through me. I can hear that cold voice murmuring something else in my ear, as she stood over my hospital bed.

"Stay away from my son."

The fog lifts, and at last I remember. *I remember that night.* And I know we've met before.

"Mrs. Porter!"

A guard jumps between the two of us, prying her away from me.

"We understand you're upset, but accosting the suspect is not acceptable—"

"She murdered my son!" Mrs. Porter shouts. "I can do whatever I want!"

I stumble backward, retreating into my cell as the guard leads her away. I slide down against the wall, leaning my head against the cool stone and letting the flood of memory wash over me.

MAY 31, 2016
JUNIOR YEAR

*A*t first I think I must be dreaming when Lana approaches me at lunch, smiling like her old self. It's been almost three weeks since we shared a table in the Dining Hall or said so much as a word to each other. She managed to convince Headmaster Higgins to change her dorm assignment in record time—I can't imagine what she had to have said about me to finagle that one—and from the moment I walked into our room and found every trace of her gone, I assumed there would be no forgiveness. Is it possible . . . could I have been wrong?

"Lana." I stand up from my new lunch table, which Brianne was nice enough to let me rejoin.

"Hi. Can we talk?"

"Of course!" I start to make room for her on the bench, but she shakes her head.

"Not here."

"Oh, yeah. Duh."

While our classmates have caught on to the rift between me and Lana, no one has a clue what it's about. Chace and I kept our promise. As far as the public knows, the two of them are still an item, and he's never looked at me twice. It's no wonder she wouldn't want us rehashing things within earshot of Brianne and the rest of orchestra.

"I'll see you in class," I tell Brianne, bending down to give her a quick hug.

She gives me a disapproving look as I join Lana, and I feel a pang of guilt. I'd hate for her to think I'm blowing her off now that Lana's talking to me again—but I also can't miss this chance to make things right.

I toss my barely-touched lunch in the trash, and Lana and I walk in awkward silence out of the dining hall, through the front doors and onto the grassy quad. She settles on a bench and I follow suit, my palms growing sweaty in anticipation.

"So I thought about everything," Lana says carefully. "And I'm still really upset, but . . . I don't hate you."

"You don't?" I let out a sigh of relief. "Really?"

"I might have done the same thing if I were in your shoes," she concedes. "Anyway, I'm still not ready to tell everyone about Chace. It's more than a little humiliating, being dumped for you."

My face reddens.

"I'm sorry—"

"But," she continues. "I think you and I can maybe try to be friends again."

"Really?" I throw my arms around her. "You don't know how much I've wished for that."

I want it so much, I don't even entertain my fleeting thought that this might all be too good to be true.

"So, remember the masquerade party I wanted to have?" Lana asks, switching topics abruptly.

"Yeah, I think so."

"It's happening tonight. We can't make it as big as my original plan, since that'll be too hard to keep quiet from Higgins, so it'll just be a small group of us girls. We'll take plenty of Instagrams, though, and make everyone else jealous." She gives me a conspiratorial smile. "You in?"

To be back in Lana's good graces and welcomed into her inner circle again, all without having to say goodbye to Chace, is more than I dared to dream. Nothing could keep me from this party.

"Definitely," I tell her. "Where is it?"

"In the woods, just past the bridge," she replies. "We needed a private spot so we can drink without getting caught, and this'll be perfect. Meet us there at nine?"

I nod, still smiling, even though she knows I've always found those woods to be the creepiest place on Oyster Bay grounds. Especially at night.

"You don't know how much this means to me, Lana. Thank you."

• • •

I'm deep within the forest of moss-covered trees, trying not to panic. The woods are still dead silent, with no sign of anyone here but me. When I reach the low cliff that splits my path in two, a sick realization dawns on me.

I turn around slowly, my flashlight bouncing its paltry glow across the trees. There it is—another note pinned to a tree. I step forward with trepidation.

DID YOU REALLY THINK I'D FORGIVE YOU? WHAT A JOKE! HOPE YOU'RE NOT STILL SCARED OF THE WOODS, BECAUSE NO ONE IS COMING FOR YOU. YOU'RE ALL ALONE, JUST LIKE YOU DESERVE TO BE.

I stagger backward, an icy chill running through my body. She lied to me. She led me into the woods alone, when she knew I'd be terrified. I'm an idiot, such an idiot for believing her about the party, for thinking we were actually friends again.

The sound of a high-pitched trill fills the air, and I scream as a yellow-eyed owl swoops down from the sky, landing on the branch closest to me. I never knew I was scared of owls, but this one, with its blood-red coloring and beady stare, is downright fearsome. I break into a run, blinded by tears as my mind struggles to process what Lana's done. And then my ankle slams into a stump and I'm howling in pain, my body rebounding backward. With a cry of shock, I feel myself falling, tumbling over a precipice. The earth scratches my face, sticks scrape along my skin, until my head hits a slab of rock—and everything turns black.

• • •

I'm lying half awake in an unfamiliar bed, surrounded by beeping machines and the sterile smell of disinfectant. I struggle to blink, and when my eyes finally flutter open, I find myself looking up at the hazy figure of an unfamiliar woman standing over me. She has glossy dark hair and eyes that remind me of someone—but somehow I know I've never seen her before in my life.

"M—Mo—" I try to call out for my mother, but I only manage a feeble croak. My head feels heavy, my body listless, like I've swallowed sleeping pills. The strange woman hastily grabs my hand, covering it in her cold palms.

"It's all right," she says, her voice low and smooth. "Don't tire yourself by trying to speak. Just listen."

There's something hypnotic about her voice, and I lean my head back against the pillows, feeling my consciousness begin to drift. But then her grip tightens on my hand.

"I know about you and my son. And it needs to stop."

My eyes snap back open. Chace's mother? What is she doing here? Where am I? And why is she looking down at me with such contempt?

"I know all about what you're pushing him to do, but if you think you can destroy my family, you're severely mistaken." Her silky voice is a sharp contrast to her threatening words. "Stay away from my son. And if you tell one other soul about the car accident—my husband and I will make sure you never speak again."

I stare up at her in horror as she wipes the scowl off her face, replacing it with a cold smile.

"Do we understand each other?"

There's a frantic pounding in my chest and I can't answer, I can't so much as move my head. The machines' beeping turns into a squeal, and I watch helplessly as Mrs. Porter slips out of the room, just before two nurses come running in.

• • •

I wake to the sound of my mother's voice, crying out in relief.

"She opened her eyes!"

I blink up at her, my eyes flickering from her familiar face to my foreign surroundings.

"What's going on?" I ask, my voice coming out thin and wobbly. I try to swallow, but it feels like a blade is stabbing at my throat. "Where am I?"

Mom hovers over me, tears running down her cheeks as she strokes my hair.

"You're in the hospital, sweetie. You were found in the woods behind the school, badly hurt. I've never been so scared in my life." She looks closer at me. "What happened to you, darling? What were you doing there?"

I lean back against the pillow, trying to remember.

"I was—it was—"

But nothing comes to mind. All I can recall is the fear, and the piercing pain. My hand flies to the left side of my face. It is covered in thick bandages.

"Am I going to be okay?" I whisper.

Mom wipes her eyes with the back of her hand.

"Yes, darling. Thank God for that."

"My violin," I burst out, with a jolt of panic. "Will I still be able to—"

"Don't worry," she interrupts. "You hurt your head badly, but the doctors assured me it won't affect your musical cognition or your ear."

"I need my Maggini," I say. "I need to know for sure."

Mom glances outside the room.

"Your friend brought it for you. I'll bring him in, but only for a few minutes. You need to take it easy."

I hear Mom's footsteps leaving the room. When I glance up, Chace Porter is standing in her place, a bouquet of flowers in one hand and my violin case in the other. A fist tightens around my heart at the sight of him.

"Nicole," he breathes. "I was so afraid I was going to lose you."

"I—" I struggle to speak, my thoughts a foggy jumble. "Your—your mom. I think I had a dream about her."

Chace smiles slightly.

"Maybe it's because you were supposed to meet her over dinner tonight. She's visiting for the weekend. We'll do it another time, when you're all better."

He sets the flowers onto the bedside table and drops the violin case, rushing to my side. But just before he can touch me, I hold up my hand to stop him.

"Is it the pain?" he asks, his brow furrowed with worry.

"I—I can't see you anymore," I blurt out.

His mouth falls open.

"What?"

"Go back to Lana, to life before me. It'll be better for everyone. I need to stay away from you." I ache to look away, but I force myself to meet his eyes, so he'll know I'm serious.

"You hurt your head," he says, his voice shaking. "It's just the head trauma talking. You don't really mean it."

"But I do," I tell him. "I may not remember what happened to me, but I know it's my . . . punishment. This never would have happened if I hadn't—if I hadn't made the mistake of wanting you."

I hear his sharp intake of breath. I shut my eyes, and when I open them again, Chace is gone. The flowers are the only sign that he was ever here.

• • •

I rise to my feet, my mind returning to the present inside my cell. Fury swells in my chest, and I kick the cold stone wall as hard as I can, until my toes are bruised purple.

I'm beginning to have an idea of what might have happened to Chace.

And there's only one person who can help me prove it.

"This way, Miss Rivera. You'll need to remove your hood."

I shrug off my jacket but keep my head down as I follow the heavyset cop through a narrow corridor and into the Visitors' Center—such an innocent, cheery name for the most depressing, guilty place.

The cop leads me to a window with a chair and a phone on either side, like something out of *CSI*. I sit down hesitantly. Now that I'm here, I'm oddly afraid of seeing her. I'm beginning to regret the hasty decision I made when I got her call. What if someone recognizes me in here? I shake my hair in front of my face, contemplating a stealth exit, when I hear the sound of chains.

Nicole shuffles toward me, flanked by two guards. She wears the hideous orange prisoner's jumpsuit, her hands in cuffs, and for a moment I flash back to the happily naive, scarless girl I first saw practicing onstage. That girl is far away now.

She manages a slight smile as she sits in front of the glass opposite me, picking up the phone next to her. I reach for mine.

"You came," she says.

Her voice sounds different, raspy—like she's been sick or crying, or both.

"You took a big risk, spending your one phone call on me," I tell her. "What made you think I would show up?"

"You might be a lot of things but you're not a monster," she says simply. "I know you feel guilty about that night in the woods, and what happened to my face. It's easier to hate me than to feel the guilt, isn't it?"

The shock pierces my chest, the phone fumbling out of my grasp. My fingers shake as I bend down to retrieve it. I thought she didn't remember. I thought my secret was safe.

"I don't know what you're talking about," I finally answer. "I—I didn't do that to your face."

"But it's because of you that I was in the woods that night and got hurt," Nicole says. "We both know you're the one who lured me there."

I should just hang up, but instead my words come tumbling out.

"I never meant for any of that to happen. I just—just wanted to show you what it feels like to have the rug pulled out from under you, like how you made me feel." I tug at a strand of hair. "If I'd known what would end up happening to you that night . . . I wouldn't have done it."

"I believe you," Nicole says. "And I'm not trying to get you in trouble. I just need your help."

"*My* help?" I raise an eyebrow at her. What is she talking about?

"I didn't just remember the accident. I remembered being in the hospital right after," she reveals. "And Chace's mom was there. She—she threatened me into staying away from Chace and keeping quiet about this family secret they had. She would have done anything to keep the truth hidden." Nicole gives me a pointed look. *"Anything."*

"Wait, what?" I stare at her through the glass, bewildered. "You think Mrs. Porter killed her own son? That's crazy. She practically lived for him."

"I don't think she did it on purpose, but . . . Chace was going to expose a cover-up from almost two years ago, the kind of thing that would have gotten the congressman kicked out of office and tarnished the family's reputation. It was a constant source of fights between them, his desire to tell the truth and his parents' desperation to keep the lie going." Nicole takes a deep breath. "I think Chace's death could have been a fight gone too far. And now Mrs. Porter is trying to pin it on me."

I shake my head.

"I really don't know about this—"

Nicole leans forward, ignoring my protest.

"We both lost, Lana. Chace is gone. I don't expect us to ever be friends again, but we both cared about him, and if we have any hope of putting this behind us, we need his real killer in here instead of me. Your mom has the power to help make that happen."

I bite my lip in guilt. She has no idea the extent of my mom's power, and how it likely helped dig Nicole further into this hole.

"So you want my mom to hunt down evidence on Mrs. Porter?" I ask.

She nods fervently.

"But what if . . . what if I have another theory?"

Nicole stares at me, as I pull out the phone Ryan swiped from the Dumpster.

"This might sound crazy, but just listen. Ryan and I were at Pete's Canteen, and we overheard Brianne yelling at someone over the phone—"

Nicole lets out an outraged sputter.

"*My* Brianne? You're not actually suggesting—"

"Let me finish," I interrupt her. "Brianne was freaking out, acting different than I'd ever seen her, and something about it gave me pause. Ryan and I followed her outside and watched her throw her phone in the Dumpster. It was so weird and dramatic . . . something just seemed *off* . . . and I made Ryan get the phone."

Nicole folds her arms across her chest, clearly more offended on Brianne's behalf than curious about what I have to say.

"*Anyway*," I continue. "We saw that it was one of those cheapo disposable phones. We redialed her last call, and it went to a guy's voice mail. A Justin Jensen."

Nicole freezes in place. I watch the color drain from her face, and realize I just might be on to something.

"Maybe it's a coincidence, but I recognized the name Jensen from what Chace said the day you guys . . . you know, had that *talk* with me. And then I remembered how I saw you wearing the silver cardigan the night of Tyler's party—but I only saw it from the back, and you weren't wearing it earlier. Could someone else have had access to your sweater? Someone we both know is close enough in height and hair color to pass for you from behind?"

Nicole's lower lip begins to quiver.

"I—I let her borrow whatever she wanted," she whispers. "She knew I kept an extra key under the mat."

I squeeze my eyes shut, hardly able to believe it, even though it was my own theory. And then Nicole gasps, covering her mouth with a trembling hand.

"*JJ*," she says, staring at me. "That was Brianne's old boyfriend. She was crazy about him, and devastated when they broke up. JJ must have been a nickname for—"

"Justin Jensen," I chime in. "But what does he have to do with Chace?"

"Justin is the one who took the fall," Nicole says. "He was

the one charged in the hit-and-run and sent away. Maybe—maybe that's why he broke up with Brianne, and why she never explained it to me. The timing all lines up."

"What hit-and-run?" I ask.

But before she can answer, the cop who escorted me in appears at my shoulder.

"You have one more minute, and then visiting hours are up."

I nod quickly, then turn back to the glass.

"Look, I've learned a few things from my mother. If Brianne really did this . . . I might be able to trick her into confessing."

• • •

At the sound of the knock, I grab my iPhone and fire off a quick text message, before shoving the phone into my bedside drawer. With a deep breath, I answer the door. *Here goes.*

"Hey, Brianne."

"Hi!" She gives me an eager smile as she walks into my room, clutching her cello case.

"Have a seat." I gesture to the bed, then turn to the mini-fridge next to my desk. "Want anything to drink?"

"No, thanks. I'm good." She perches on the edge of my bed. "It was so nice of you and your mom to think of me. I have to say, I got pretty excited when I saw your text."

I try not to smirk.

"Yeah, well, Nicole was such a hit when she performed at

the New Year's party last year, that my mom was hoping for a repeat performance. But obviously now we need a different performer, so I thought of you."

Brianne nods.

"Well, I'm more than up to the task. Does the congresswoman have a particular piece in mind? I brought a list of songs that are great for solo cello—"

"Oh, we can go over song selection in a minute," I say breezily. "I wanted to actually talk to you about something private first." I give her my best secretive look, and she leans in.

"Yeah? What about?"

"Nicole."

I watch as Brianne stiffens. Her smile sticks to her face, like a mask.

"What about her?"

"I wanted to thank you," I say. "For getting her out of my life."

Brianne tilts her head up at me, frowning.

"Um, what did *I* do?"

Here it comes. I take another deep breath before delivering the blow.

"You framed Nicole for Chace's murder, didn't you? It was brilliant."

Brianne leaps up from the bed, stumbling over her cello case in her haste.

"Are you crazy? What are you *talking* about?"

I open my desk drawer and retrieve the disposable phone. Brianne's face turns a ghastly shade of pale.

"It's okay," I say soothingly. "It's just us here. And because of you, the girl who stabbed me in the back is behind bars."

"Who—" Brianne gulps, beads of sweat dotting her pale, pointy face. "Who else have you told about this?"

"Which part? How you killed Chace to get revenge for the guy you're obsessed with? Or how you wore Nicole's sweater, wrote an incriminating email from her account, and planted the murder weapon in her room?"

"Shut up, shut *up*!" Brianne's eyes flash wildly. I can see the killer in them now. But I'm not afraid.

"Why did you do it, Brianne? There's no use denying what I know. Plus, I'm on your side," I tell her. "If you knew enough to frame Nicole, you obviously know what she did to me, and that Chace and I weren't really together in the end. You can have my silence—if you just tell me why."

Brianne's eyes dart between me and the door, and I hold my breath, waiting for her to crack. When she finally speaks, her voice is markedly different from the girl I go to school with and thought I knew. Her tone is flat and harsh, her eyes deadened, like whatever bit of soul she had left just slipped away.

"He ruined it. Chace Porter ruined everything."

"What did he do?" I urge her on.

She sinks to the floor, the fight draining from her as she buries her head against her knees.

"You don't know what JJ—Justin—meant to me. He was my everything. We were supposed to move in together after graduation, we had all these plans. And then he just up and disappeared a year ago. He broke up with me with no explanation. I went crazy wondering. I never got over it." Brianne meets my eyes. "I finally heard from him two weeks ago. He must have felt guilty for ignoring all my texts and emails, because he—he came to visit me and eventually told me everything, how Chace's parents bribed the Jensens into making Justin take the blame for a car accident Chace caused. He didn't just disappear on me. He was sent to juvie." Brianne wipes her eyes roughly. "I thought maybe we could start things up again and that's why he was back, but *no*. Justin was leaving me again. His parents found a way for him to have a fresh start and a clean reputation—in Canada. I offered to go with him, but he said no, that he was only here for a proper goodbye, to give me *closure*." She spits the word.

"So then what?" I prod. "You decided to take your anger out on Chace?"

Brianne shakes her head wildly.

"I didn't plan anything. It—it was an accident. I went to the party to confront Chace, and then I saw the knife in Tyler's kitchen and figured I'd just—I don't know, scare Chace a little, get him to call the police and clear Justin's name so he could come home and be with me again. But then when I told him what I knew and he admitted it all, something in me just . . ." Brianne swallows hard. "Snapped. I got so angry seeing him standing there, the so-called *star* of the school who made the past year hell for Justin and me. I'd never experienced anger like that in my life." Brianne's voice lowers to a chilling whisper. "I didn't even see the knife go in. It just . . . happened."

I close my eyes, digging my fingernails into my palm as I try to fight the sickening images playing in my mind.

"And how—how did you know to frame Nicole for it?" I ask, forcing myself to continue drawing the story out of her. "I saw you getting fingerprinted. How did you pull this off?"

Brianne narrows her eyes.

"I'm not an idiot. I knew to hold the knife through a napkin so I wouldn't get my prints on it. And I'm also not as slow as Nicole thought. It was clear what was going on between them. The only times Chace ever spoke to me was to ask about her, and then there was your mysterious falling-out. It was so obvious." Brianne looks away. "I didn't set out to hurt Nicole, but I had to protect myself. She was the obvious suspect. Plus, if anyone can understand putting yourself first, it's Nicole. She just *takes* everything, from the Philharmonic showcase and Juilliard, to your boyfriend." Brianne gives me a meaningful look, as if the two of us are in this together, and it's all I can do to refrain from hitting her.

"Well, I guess you're about to find out how understanding she and everyone else will be."

Brianne's head whips up.

"What?"

"Right about *now!*" I shout my cue, and the door flies open. I stifle a smile as Detective Kimble, Officer Ladge, and two backup cops march into the room.

"You—you set me up!" Brianne shrieks, her mouth falling open in disbelief.

"You have the right to remain silent," Detective Kimble begins to recite as Officer Ladge pins her to the wall. I grab my iPhone from the bedside drawer.

"Here." I hand it to the detective as the cops drag Brianne out of the room, screaming in protest. "I recorded her confession."

Detective Kimble places her hand on my shoulder, looking into my eyes.

"You did a very good thing, Lana. Because of you, an innocent girl is being set free."

"I know," I reply. "I never imagined I'd ever want to help Nicole Morgan. But I'm glad I did it."

And I'm glad, too, that Nicole was right about me. I'm not a monster. And now I'm letting all of this go. For good.

26

NICOLE

I can hear them leading her to her cell. Her chains jangle as she flails and kicks, her screams penetrating the walls. A girl like Brianne Daly, from a proper, upper-class family, never imagined herself in a place like this, and she'll never stop fighting it. But this is one fight she'll lose. If there's anything I can trust, it's that the Porters will stop at nothing to ensure their son's killer stays behind bars.

"Miss Morgan? It's time."

I glance up and smile. Wes, the only friendly guard on the prison's staff, is the one escorting me out today.

I rise to my feet, closing my eyes and letting the relief flood through me, as Wes opens the door to my cell. I follow him out and I don't look back.

My breath is lodged somewhere between my heart and my throat as we walk through the corridor of cells, and I wonder if I'm going to see her. That's when I hear a guttural cry, and I turn.

Brianne's hands grip the bars of her cell. Her body shudders as she watches me, walking out a free woman.

"How could you do it, Brianne?" I whisper. This truth is too painful. *"How?"*

But she doesn't answer. Wes gently pushes me forward, leaving everything that's rotten behind.

There's a swarm of reporters waiting as I appear at the top of the jailhouse stairs, ready to descend to my freedom. But this time, I'm not hiding from their flashbulbs or shouted questions. I break into a smile when I see Mom and John Sanford, Mom leaping up the steps two at a time to get to me, and I fling myself into her arms.

"My client would like to make a statement," John Sanford says, after I give him a nod to let him know I'm ready.

An uncharacteristic hush comes over the crowd. Dozens of microphones point in my direction. I take a deep breath.

"I want to thank the people who believed in my innocence. It was easy for so many of you to assume I was guilty, just because I maybe looked the part, or because I come from a single-parent home, or that I was the so-called jilted lover, or whatever stereotypes were being tossed around. But the snap judgments were all so wrong." I meet the eyes of the different reporters and am gratified to see a few of them looking away in chagrin. "Yet I made a mistake in judgment, too. The

friend I trusted most is the one who did the unthinkable—
while the last person I expected to help me is the one who
proved my innocence. I want to thank Lana Rivera, with all
my heart."

There's a smattering of applause, and I smile.

"For the last few weeks, you've known me as someone
I'm not. 'The Girl in the Picture,' or 'The Phantom of the
Philharmonic.' It's a joke to all of you, but this is my life. And
from now on, I'm determined that you will know me for the
right reasons. For my music."

As I finish, a breeze wraps me in its embrace. And I know
it's him—saying goodbye.

EPILOGUE

CHACE

I can still see her sometimes. I may have passed on and stepped through the proverbial pearly gates, but a part of me is still back there with her. I know she feels me, too. I can tell by the way she looks up to the sky when she plays her violin. Like she knows I'm there—like she's playing for me.

Even up here it's possible to torture myself, obsessing over what might have been if we had all simply told the truth from the beginning. If Nicole had admitted her feelings for me from the start, we could have been together from day one. If I had gone against my parents and told the truth about the car accident, I would still be alive. But then I never would have gone to Oyster Bay. That's the rub. I wouldn't have met her.

My Nicole is a star now, playing to ever-growing crowds. Sometimes her old friend Damien Bell joins her on cello; other times she plays alongside a world-famous musician, like the pianist Grigory Sokolov. But it doesn't matter who's on-stage with her—she's the one they're all looking at.

No matter what kind of concert it is, Nicole always, without fail, plays the songs she knows I want to hear. "Tomorrow Is My Turn." "Lovesong." "Summertime." Those are for me. They're ours.

One day, many years from now, I know we'll be together again. Until then, I wait.

I listen.

Acknowledgments

None of this would be possible without the love, support, and encouragement of my incredible parents: my father, aka my first and forever love (FAFL!), Shon Saleh, and my mother/best friend/angel on earth, ZaZa Saleh. I am so grateful to you both for going above and beyond to nurture my dreams ever since I was a little girl, and for your constant belief in me. Thank you for reading every draft of my every idea, for being the best parents and friends I could wish for, and for giving me a life filled with love.

To the readers: Thank you for bringing meaning to my every story. This is for you!

It's such a wonderful feeling to be publishing my fourth novel, and I have two amazing women to thank for this dream come true: my editor, Krista Vitola, and publisher, Beverly Horowitz. Thank you for steering me so wisely, and for believing in *Girl in the Picture* when it was just a seed of an idea. Beverly, your continued support and guidance truly means the world. Krista, your editorial brilliance helped me take this book so many notches above the first draft, and I'm grateful to work with someone as smart and talented as you. Book #4 has been a blast—I can't wait for our next one!

Thank you to everyone at Penguin Random House who has blessed this book with their skills: Dan for stunning cover design, Annette Szlachta-McGinn and Colleen Fellingham for their copyediting wizardry, Marketing and Cassie McGinty in Publicity for spreading the word about the book, and Jocelyn Lange for bringing it to foreign shores. I am thankful for all of you!

Many thanks to the world's best agents: Greg Pedicin, Joe Veltre, and Lynn Fimberg at Gersh. I am so grateful for your support and guidance with all the projects cooking in my brain! You guys are wizards. And thank you to my awesome lawyer, Chad Christopher, who not only introduced me to this dream team but is also such an invaluable part of it.

Brooklyn Weaver, I can't thank you enough for reading this book and deciding to sign me and change my life. Thank you for dreaming big dreams for my writing and pushing to make them come true! ☺ I'm forever grateful, and so happy to be with Energy Entertainment!

Thank you to the booksellers and librarians across the country who shared my books with readers and invited me to visit. I couldn't do any of this without all of you!

Many thanks to my fellow YA authors, especially Kara Thomas, for honoring me with a wonderful blurb, and Jessica Brody, Colleen Houck, and Amy Plum for being so vocally supportive of my books—it means a lot coming from you writing dynamos!

So much love and thanks to my truly awesome big brother, Arian Saleh, for fostering my imagination while at the same time keeping me grounded with your love and friendship. And thank you for giving me a sister I adore, Sainaz Saleh!

To my incredible family, the Salehs and Majidis—I love you beyond words! And lots of love to my in-laws, Dottie and the Robertiellos!

To my family members in heaven: Papa and Mama Monir, Jimmy, and Honey: I love you forever and am so grateful for your influence on my life.

So much love and thanks to my honorary big sister (and maid of honor!), Brooke Kaufman Halsband. Your belief in me all those years ago was a life-changer, and there aren't enough words in the dictionary for how grateful I am for your unwavering support and your incredible heart!

Heather Holley: producer, songwriting partner, kindred spirit, friend, and matchmaker! From the day we met, my world grew so much bigger, and I am so thankful for you.

Josh Bratman, thank you for championing my writing in such a huge way and helping me make one of my biggest dreams come true. I'm a better writer because of your insightful notes, and a happier human thanks to having you, Alex, Jordy, and the Bratman kids in my life.

Special thanks to Alex, Josh, and Jordy Bratman for your wonderful friendship and support. You guys are like family, and I thank you for welcoming me into yours!

Thank you to Chessa Donaldson for reading practically everything I've written since we met, and for your helpful feedback! Lots of love to you and Ross, as well as Dan and Heather Kiger, Jon and Emily Sandler, Alex and Lisa Tse, Mike and Seema Pietrocarlo, and the rest of the amazing group that I'm so lucky to have married into.

Many thanks to my girls for your incredible friendship and for encouraging all my projects and dreams. Mia Antonelli, you are a true MVP when it comes to friendship! Roxane Cohanim and Adriana Ameri, the fact that we grew up together and have stayed so close is one of the most special things in life. Kirsten Guenther, Marise Freitas, Ami and Mayu McCartt, Camilla Moshayedi, Dani Cordaro, Christina Harmon—I love and thank you all!

And to the person who has my heart forever, my husband, Chris Robertiello: you are a constant reminder that dreams come true. I am so grateful for you, and for our beautiful life together with Daisy!

About the Author

ALEXANDRA MONIR is the author of the popular time-travel YA novel *Timeless*, as well as its sequel, *Timekeeper*, and a romantic thriller, *Suspicion*. She is also a professional recording artist and composer. Alexandra and her husband live in Los Angeles, where she is at work on her next novel while also composing an original musical. Her music is available on iTunes, and you can follow her on Twitter at @TimelessAlex.